The Assassin of Irolyth

Willow Asteria

THE
ASSASSIN
OF
IROLYTH
A REALMS OF ELSWYTH STANDALONE
WILLOW ASTERIA

Content Warning

Please be advised that this book may not be suitable for all audiences.

This book contains sexual content, execution by hanging, death, blood, loss of a family member, graphic violence, and other topics some readers may not find suitable.

Realms of Elswyth

In the land of Elswyth, six portals exist that lead to the fae realms.

Orilon. Irolyth. Alari. Aeros. Khaldon. Tarak.

ELSWYTH
THE HUMAN REALM
VARIA
ZAMORA
MAGLA
PENDRIL
CALDOR
PORTAL
TO
ANOTHER REALM

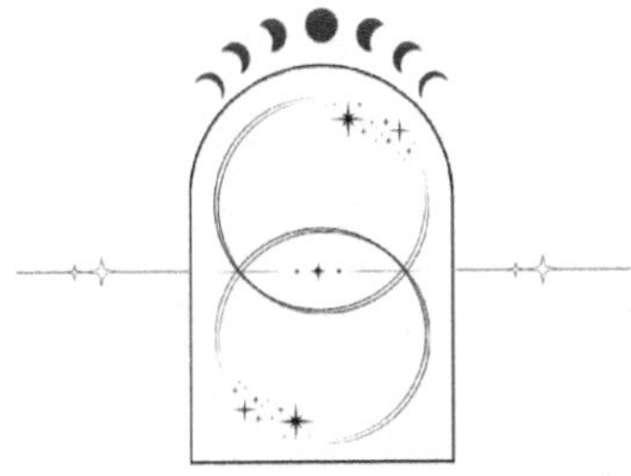

One

I pressed my back to the wall, hoping the guards in the attached corridor wouldn't see me as they rushed past. Ringing filled my ears, and my heart pounded in my chest. Lucky for me, they continued down the hall, with not a clue I was so close by. Once they were out of view, I rushed into the secret passage that left the castle.

I had to escape. If they found me, it would mean my end. There was not a single second I could afford to waste. My feet ached as I ran through the stone passageway.

After what seemed like an eternity, I found the trap door exit. Climbing the ladder, I opened the hatch and climbed out. The bright midday sun caused my eyes to squint. Now, I stood in front of the castle, just outside of the pale stone wall. Just in front of the gates, a stage had been set. The royal family hung from the gallows for the realm to see. Blood dripped from the queen's back onto the ground below her. Her orange and white wings had been ripped from her and tossed on the ground below.

I could not stop to pay my respects. I could not stop to say my goodbyes. I could not stop and let the weight of the world crush me.

Wrapping my tan cloak tighter around me, I pulled on my hood concealing my auburn locks, and disappeared into the woods just outside the wall that surrounded the castle. To my surprise, the new king already had guards searching the forest. I figured he would have focused all of his attention inside of the castle. Their angry voices echoed through the trees, but no matter where I looked, I could not tell where they were coming from.

"Any sign of the princess?" One of them called out.

"She's just a girl. There's no way she was included in this treason," another said.

My body tensed as I crouched behind a thick bush. Sending a prayer up to The Mother, I hoped they would not find me. Peeking through the leaves, I saw the two men as they argued.

"Are you saying King Joffrey is lying?" His voice was filled with venom.

"I just don't know how a sixteen-year-old girl could be a part of something so sinister."

"She has the royal flames like the rest of them. None of them can be trusted!"

They were too focused on each other to notice me. Quietly, I continued to move through the forest, hoping to get away from them.

"King Joffrey is Klaus' brother. How do we know he doesn't have the flames as well?"

I tucked behind a large redwood tree, listening to the two men argue, holding my breath when they mentioned King Klaus. He was a kind and fair king. All his people loved him, until his brother, Joffrey, claimed the royal flames were the cause of a sacred temple's destruction. Quickly, the people of Irolyth turned against Klaus and the rest of the royal family. How could the people who once loved King Klaus turn on him so quickly? Joffrey did not even give the Royal Family a chance to defend themselves against the allegations before he hunted them down to have them executed.

"Are you trying to say our new king is evil?"

"All I'm saying is we shouldn't rush to send a child to her death. It's bad enough one child was already killed."

There was silence for a moment, and I peeked around the tree to see if they were still nearby. I watched in horror as one of them quickly slit the other's throat. His body hit the ground before a sound could escape his lips.

"One less traitor to deal with," the first man said in a cold tone. He then turned away, walking in the opposite direction. The body was left on the forest floor in a puddle of blood.

Before he could find me, I ventured deeper into the woods and headed south toward the bog. I ran as fast as I could, ignoring the pain in my body as I pushed it beyond its limits. In the mire's center, I would find my refuge.

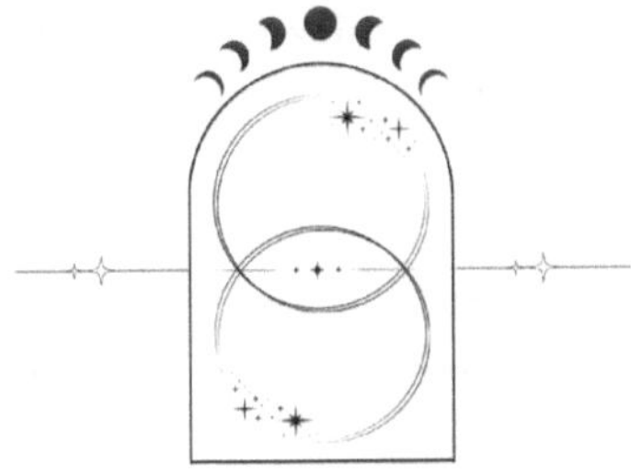

Two

"Piper! Fetch me another ale!" A patron yelled from the other side of the bar. He was an older man, about in his mid-forties. He and his friends came to The White Rabbit every Wednesday night to play a few rounds of darts, drink some ale, and enjoy the music the bards played. Other than them, the tavern was dead, compared to a Friday or Saturday night when this place was packed.

I took a deep breath. "Right away, Clarence." I put down the cleaning cloth I was using to wipe down the bar top, washed my hands, and poured him a new mug of ale. When I sat it down in front of him, I offered a soft smile. "This is your last one for tonight. Remember, you told me to cut you off at three."

"Damn, am I at three already?" He let out a joyous laugh. "Well, let me pay my tab, and once me and the boys are done with this round, we'll be out of your hair." He pulled out his wallet and removed a sizable amount of money.

Before I even counted it, I spoke. "Even if you were buying for all your friends tonight, this is way too much."

"The rest is your tip for putting up with us. Don't think we haven't noticed you stay open late on Wednesdays to accommodate us."

I counted the money, put the amount for the ales into the register, and tucked the remainder in my front pocket. "Thank you. You guys don't rush this last game. I'm betting on you to win."

He took his ale with a final laugh and returned to his friends. I continued my cleaning duties as Stephanie, the owner of The White Rabbit, approached.

"The city officials stopped by again this morning," she said as she leaned against the bar.

My eyes slowly lifted to meet hers. "And?" My heart pounded in my chest and my fist tightened around the cleaning cloth.

"Your paperwork is all filed. They believed the documents I forged. You are officially a citizen of Elswyth."

I released the breath I was holding, and tears filled my eyes. "Really?"

She nodded. "My little firecracker, you are home." A smile grew across her face.

Rushing over, I wrapped her in a hug and sobbed. After three years, I finally found somewhere I could call home. I had gone to a place where Joffrey would never find me. I now lived in the capital city of Elswyth, the human realm. For the first year I lived in Zamora, I stayed in hostels if there was room. I was lucky to meet Steph. She offered me a job, a room, and a friend. I lived on the third floor of the tavern. It was just a small one-bedroom apartment, but it meant everything to me.

"Thank you so much!"

She squeezed me tighter. "Why don't you call it a night? I'll wrap up here."

I wished her, and the guys, a good night before rushing upstairs. Once the door was shut behind me, I snapped my fingers, and the fireplace set ablaze. I went into the kitchen and found a note on the counter.

Check the ice box.

-Steph

I opened the ice chest and saw a box of my favorite cupcakes from a bakery across the city. Lemon cake filled with curd frosted with marshmallow icing with the top lightly torched. Taking the whole dozen, I sat on the couch in front of the fireplace. One by one I ate half the box while reading one of my favorite books.

For the first time in three years, I could truly relax.

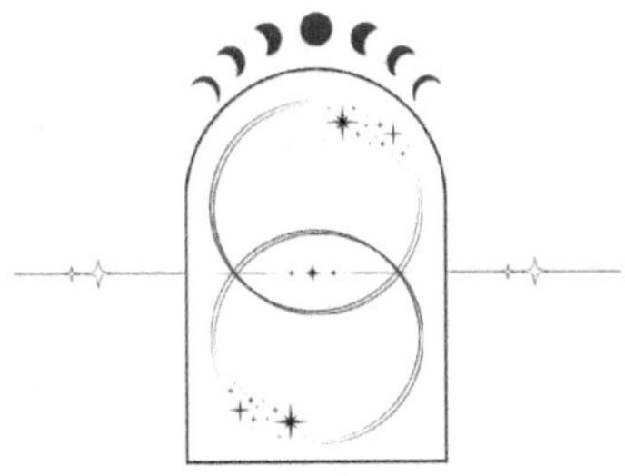

Three

That Friday, The White Rabbit was packed. I could barely catch a break as customers continued ordering drinks while Steve, my co-worker, took food orders and delivered them to the guests. If you had asked me three years ago before I ran from Irolyth, I would have laughed if you had told me I'd be working as a bartender in the human realm. This life was so different from my life back home, but this was the small life I longed for.

No longer was my day planned down to the letter. No longer was I watching my every movement. No longer was I stuck in a life that wasn't mine.

In the crowd, a tall, slender man faced away from me. Breath caught in my throat as I stared at his auburn hair. How could he be here? Did Joffrey really travel through the portal into the human realm to find me himself? He turned, and I exhaled in relief as it was a young man's brown eyes staring back at me.

I heard Steve say something, but couldn't understand the words. When I turned to face him, concern was seeded in his hazel eyes.

"I'm sorry. What did you say?" I asked.

"Are you ok? You just got paler than normal, and that's saying something for you."

"I am not really feeling good. All of a sudden I got really hot," I lied. Steve did not know the truth of where I came from. I could not tell him that I thought I saw a fae king who wanted me dead.

"Go step out back. I will take care of things for a bit. Get some fresh air."

"Are you sure?" I looked around the bar full of people. Several wanted drinks, and the chef in the back just called for a food runner.

"Go, before I change my mind." He motioned to the door that led to the back of house.

I quickly made my way through the kitchens, grabbing a glass of water before I walked outside to the alley and sat on the step. Chugging the water, I tried to gather my thoughts. No matter how much I told myself I was safe, I wasn't. I would never be as free as I wanted to be. That monster would haunt me for the rest of my life. There was nowhere I could hide from him. Nowhere was safe. Who was to say he didn't already send people through the portal to try to find me?

I allowed the cool air to calm me before returning to work. The White Rabbit now had much fewer people in it than before. I looked over at Steve as he made his way from a table in the back corner of the tavern. It was he who now looked pale as a ghost, a stark contrast to his normally tan skin.

As he poured a mug of ale, he gave me the side eye. "Whatever you do, do *not* go over to that table. I will handle it," he said in a low tone.

A shiver ran down my spine. Never had Steve spoken to me that way. "Why? Who is that?" I asked as I peered past him. A lone man sat at the table with short, spiked black hair, a five o'clock shadow gracing his chiseled jaw, and piercing gray eyes. For the first time, I found a human man to be attractive. Steve stepped in front of me and blocked my view from him.

"That is a very dangerous man, and Steph would have my ass if something happened to you. Please, just listen to me about this."

Before I could respond, I heard a voice like velvet. "I plan on being in this part of the city for a few days. Are there any rooms available?"

The man leaned against the bar. The sleeves of his dark shirt were rolled up and revealed two lean, tat-tooed arms.

"No vacancy," Steve spat.

"Now, I know that isn't true. I heard several people cancel their rooms after I walked into the bar. What a pity to lose out on that much money. You wouldn't want to lose out on any more, would you?" Those gray eyes darkened as he spoke. His gaze met mine, and he offered a predatory grin as he looked me over. "Well, hello there. What a pretty little thing *you* are."

Heat flushed my cheeks. There was something about him that lured me in. Steve responded to the man before I could. "Do not speak to her. You can stay here, but I don't want to catch you looking in her direction. Do you understand?"

"Oh, Steve," a dark chuckle escaped his lips. "Do you think just because you got out of the business that you are better than me? Do you *really* think you can tell me what to do? Do not make me remind you of your place, especially in front of your little friend here. Now, what is my room number?"

Steve swallowed hard and clenched his fists so tight I could see the whites of his knuckles. "204," he said through his teeth.

"See, that wasn't so hard." The man reached across the counter, grabbed the ale Steve had poured before the confrontation, and headed back to his table.

"What did he mean by you being 'out of the busi-ness'?" I questioned.

"You have your secrets, Piper, and I have mine. Go upstairs to your apartment. Do not open the door for anyone unless it's me or Steph. Understood?"

"But the bar isn't closed," I protested.

"Yes, it is. Now go. Do not argue with me on this," he said with such venom it nearly caused me to stagger back.

In the two years I had known Steve, he was always a kind soul. The man that I saw before me was not someone I recognized. But he was right, we both had our secrets, and I would not want him prying into mine.

I nodded and headed for the stairs. As I passed the mystery man's table, our eyes locked. He gave me a flirty wink before I looked away and ran upstairs.

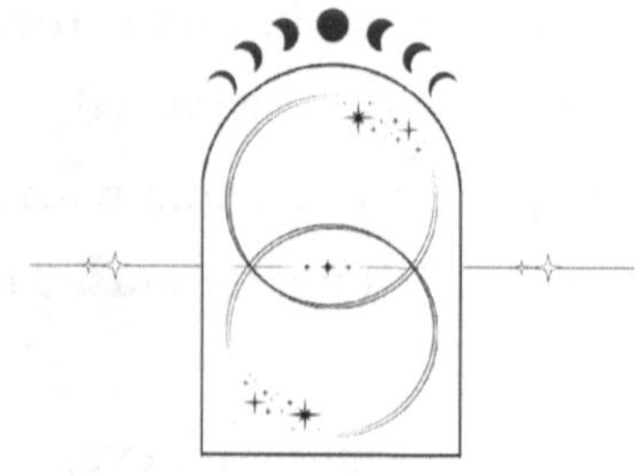

Four

The next morning, I awoke to a pounding on my door. I got out of bed, wrapped my silk robe around my body, and peered through the peephole. Steph stood on the other side, steadily pounding on the door, so I yanked it open.

"Where is the fire? What's going on?" I asked. Never had she come to me so panicked. I was worried the building was on fire.

"Oh, thank the heavens." She let out a sigh of relief and wrapped me in a tight hug. Stunned, I stood there frozen in her embrace. What was wrong with her? "Steve told me what happened last night."

"He wouldn't tell me who that man was. He just told me to stay away, and I listened." All night, I had been kept up by the thought of our new guest. Why was he so dangerous, and how did Steve know him?

She finally released me and headed for the couch, her long, blonde hair flowing behind her as she walked. "His name is Jax. A well-known assassin in the city. Extremely dangerous. I want you to take the next few days off just until he's gone. Steve is right. You shouldn't be around him."

Fear radiated through my body. His name was very well known in Zamora. Jax was credited with assassinating several high-ranking officials in Elswyth, as well as anyone else who got in his way. To decline him from staying here would have been the death of all of us.

"Understood. Just let me know when I can come back to work."

"I will, and you'll still get paid for this time."

I sat down next to her on the couch. "Do you think..." I trailed off, not daring to speak the words. Was the assassin sent by Joffrey? Could this human assassin be more than what meets the eye? If I could parade as a human, so could other fae.

"It would be impossible," she said.

Stephanie was the only one I had told my secret. When I first started working for her, she promised she would protect me from whatever I was running from. She told me a secret of her own, that she was from a line of sorceresses scattered throughout Elswyth. Magic had been forbidden by the king. Over twenty years ago, he had many of the sorceresses executed just for being born with magic. I knew she was going to keep my secret, and she knew I would keep hers.

"I have to get back downstairs and keep an eye on our guest." She walked over to the door and offered me a smile. "Stay safe, my little firecracker." With that, she walked out the door, and shut it behind her.

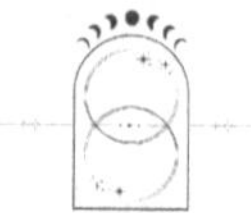

Later that night, I headed back to The White Rabbit after dining at a restaurant. I had the most delicious, spiced chicken on pita bread, with a side of dill cucumber sauce. It was the first time I tried Alivander's, and I would definitely be returning to try more of their selections. Approaching the alley where the back entrance to The White Rabbit was, I heard that familiar velvet-like voice.

"I am in between jobs right now. If you know anyone looking for work, let me know."

I took a few steps back and pressed my back against the brick wall so I could continue to eavesdrop. All day

I had fought myself on approaching Jax. If he was able to kill as many officials as he had, could he kill a king?

Would he?

"I will see what's going on within the city districts and get back to you," a rough-voiced male said.

A few seconds later, a tall, muscular man exited the alley. I quickly pushed off the wall before he looked in my direction and acted as if I was just out for a stroll. He stopped for a moment and fixed his gaze on me. The scar across his eye and his angry demeanor told me that this was a man not to fuck with. The man turned and walked away as if my presence was no concern to him.

I took a deep breath and waited until he turned the corner, then I slipped into the alley. Jax leaned against the wall with a cigarette in between his pointer and middle finger. He brought it to his lips, took a drag, and as he let out the smoke, his eyes fell on me.

"Well, well, well," he said with a grin. "I didn't expect to see you in an alley. Do you perhaps have a second job here? If so, I have an offer for you." He chuckled as he brought the cigarette back to his lips.

Disgusting. How dare he imply I was a lady of the night? I swallowed my pride and reminded myself why I was here. I leaned against the wall directly across from him. "Perhaps I have a job for you," I countered.

He kicked off the wall and strode toward me. "You do?"

"Are you as good as they say you are?"

He laughed, took another hit, and turned his head to blow the smoke away from me. Before he spoke, he threw the cigarette on the ground and snuffed it out with his boot. "Better." He winked.

"They say you are the best, but what I need you to do, I need you to be better than the best."

He lifted his arm and pressed his palm against the wall above my head. "I will be as good as you need me to be, for the right price."

"I can't pay you until after the job is done. The person I need... removed is holding all of my wealth." I looked up at him, and for the first time, noticed just how much taller he was than me. I tried to push down how intimidated I felt. If I was human, I would be terrified, but I was thankful to have magic as my protection.

Jax laughed. "Well, I don't work for free, sweet heart. If you don't have money," he gave me an up-and-down look, "I could think of other ways for you to pay me."

My throat bobbed as he leaned in, and I took in his tobacco and citrus scent. "Over my dead body," I snarled.

"Feisty and has self-respect. I like that." He leaned in close, so our gazes met. "Tell ya what. Kiss me, and I will do it without upfront payment."

Heat rose to my cheeks. "K--kiss you?" I stumbled over my words, truly shocked.

"You do know what a kiss is? Don't you?"

"I do..." Only one other time I had kissed another. It was just after I had turned thirteen. Thinking back on it now, I could still remember her soft lips on mine. She was a noble from Khaldon, another of the fae realms. The fae of Khaldon rarely left their realm, and she and her parents only stayed with us for two short months. I always wondered if Briella had stayed, would the feelings we had blossomed into love?

I tucked away the memory and focused on the assassin whose lips were dangerously close to mine.

"Well, then I don't need to explain it to you. Do we have a bargain?" His voice darkened, and I nearly melted.

"You don't even know the details of the job." The wheels turned in my head. Bargains with the fae were life-bound contracts. If I could trick him into one, he would have to help me.

"I don't need to. Whatever you need, it's worth it. Just for a kiss."

"A bargain with me is impossible to back out of," I warned. As much as I needed his help, I had to give him the chance to walk away. This was not my first bargain, but it was indeed my most dangerous.

He lifted his other hand and tucked my hair behind my ear. "I never back away from a challenge. Kiss me, and I will be your sword."

Without another word, I leaned forward, pressed my lips into his, and saw stars.

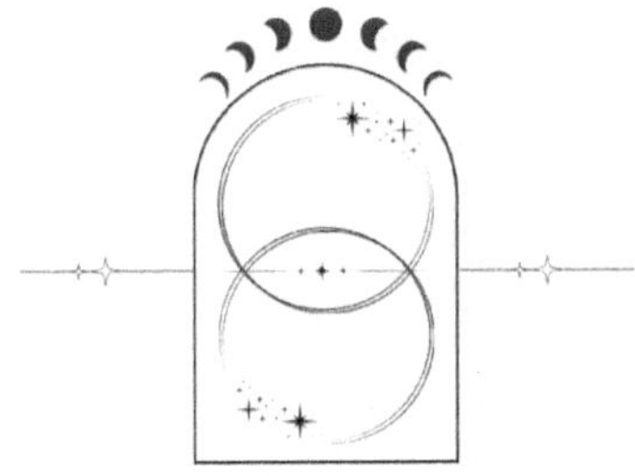

Five

The ground shook beneath our feet, and Jax staggered back.

"What was that?" His stormy eyes looked at me with a mix of confusion and fear as the tremors stopped.

"I told you. A bargain with me was serious," I said as I took a step toward him.

"What are you?" His gaze narrowed, and his back straightened as he closed the gap between us once again.

"My true name is Piper Camilla Rossi, Princess of Irolyth." Now sure he wasn't working for Joffrey, I knew it was safe to reveal myself to him. Especially since he made a deal that bound himself to my service.

"Irolyth? I have never heard of such a place." He raised his eyebrow at me.

"You wouldn't unless you were familiar with the fae." I dropped my glamour and watched his eyes widen. No longer was I a human girl with rounded ears. What now stood before the assassin was a fae princess. In my human disguise, my eyes were a dull brown, but now they were a bright emerald. My ears were now elongated and pointed. With the glamour, I was attractive to human standards. In my fae form, I was the epitome of beauty.

"I...... I thought fae only existed in the south and were horrid creatures." He stumbled over his words. His gaze darted around the alley as if he were expecting those monsters to crawl out of the shadows.

"Those are the cursed fae of Orilon. There are six fae realms that you can get to from the portals hidden throughout Elswyth." My heart broke as I thought of those cursed people. Many years ago, the fae of Orilon had angered a sorceress, and she had cursed their people to turn into horrid gray creatures with bat-like wings. Losing all their control, they now had a blood lust that could not be satisfied. Stories of their ruthless behavior had traveled through Elswyth. No one was dumb enough to travel southwest and risk being torn apart by their massive claws. The poor city of Pendril was left to its own devices to defend itself against any that found their way through the portal.

"If you are a fae princess, why do you need to work at The White Rabbit? Why hire a human assassin?" His gaze focused on me and crossed his arms in front of him.

"My uncle killed my family and stole the throne. I need you to kill him so I can reclaim my kingdom." Tears welled in my eyes as the image of my family hung for the kingdom to see flashed through my mind. I missed them every day.

"You think I can kill a fae king?" He scoffed.

"You said you were the best. You have killed several high-ranking officials. If anyone can, it's you. Besides, you made a bargain, you have to see it through."

"And if I don't? What happens if I back out now?"

"You die," I said in a cold tone. "There is no backing out until we are done."

"You can't be serious. Release me from the bargain now!"

"What's done is done. How long will you need to prepare?"

Jax turned and clenched his fists. He let out a low grumble before he spoke. "Give me three days."

"You better return."

"Not like I have a choice." He snarled as he walked out of the alley.

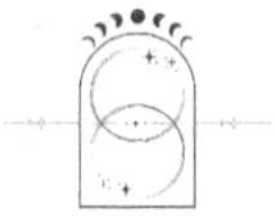

The next morning, I found Steph and Steve sitting at a table in the corner of the bar's kitchen speaking in hushed tones. Their eyes were glued to me as I joined them.

"Jax wasn't in his room this morning," Steve said, with worry in his voice.

"No. He wasn't. He will return, however," I said as I grabbed the carafe of coffee and poured myself a mug. I added three sugar cubes and a splash of cream.

"How do you know?" Steph asked with a lift of her brow.

"He and I will be leaving together when he returns. We struck a deal. He is going to help me return home." I took a sip of my coffee and it warmed my core.

Steph's eyes widened as she understood my meaning. Her mouth fell open, but no words escaped.

Anger contorted Steve's face. "How is he going to help you? Don't you remember me telling you to stay away?"

"He's the only one who can." I took a sip of my coffee, avoiding Steve's gaze. I may have the royal flames, but I swore I saw fire in his eyes.

"I don't understand. Why are you leaving with him?" He slammed his fist against the table, making the dishes clatter.

Steph reached across the table and placed her hand on top of his. "It is not for you to understand. This is a journey Piper must face." Sadness welled in her eyes. "My little firecracker, I will miss you. I understand why you must go, but, gods, I will miss you."

"I owe it to my family," I said as tears welled in my eyes. "I need to get my home back."

Steph stood and wrapped me in a hug. "Heavy is the head that wears the crown. When you are queen, don't forget about us," she whispered in my ear.

I hugged her back, just as tight. "I will never forget you. For you are the greatest friendship I have ever known."

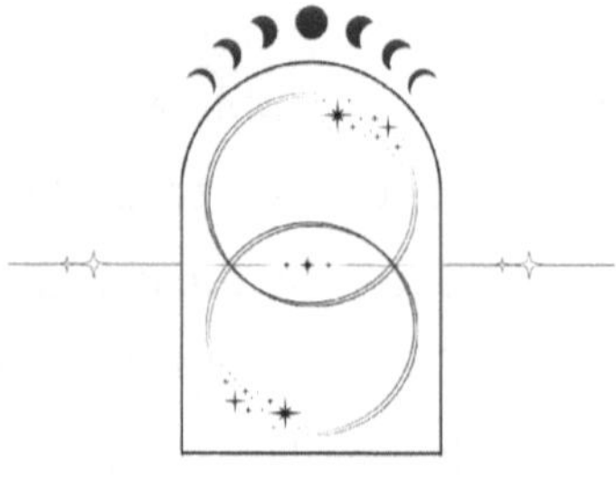

Six

As promised, Jax returned three days after his depar-
ture. Stephanie had closed The White Rabbit for the
past few days so we could spend our last moments together. The two of them had truly become my family
these past years, and I would miss them greatly.

But Stephanie was right. Heavy is the head that wears
the crown. Once I returned to Irolyth and reclaimed the
throne, I would be queen. I owed it to my family and
kingdom to give them the monarch they deserved. Anyone who would slaughter their kin for power should not
possess it. It was time I grew up and stopped being a
coward.

I prayed to The Mother I would make my family
proud. Queen was never a title I was meant to hold.

The next monarch was supposed to be my twin brother, Alexander. He spent his entire life training for that moment. I was just a trophy for my parents. A pretty little doll to make sure the royal family looked perfect to the kingdom. Never was I taught anything that would be useful for ruling. I knew my fate would have been to be married off to another fae royal for political gain.

Though the six fae realms were separate, we were all tied politically for one reason or another.

Jax was leaning against the bar that evening when I had come down to wish Steph and Steve my final goodbye. He wore tight black pants and a black T-shirt. I couldn't help but to further examine the tattoos gracing his arms. They were swirls of darkness, almost like shadows.

"So where exactly are we going, *princess*?" He asked with a snarl at the last word.

I shot him a glare. "We need to head to the back alley and into the sewers."

Jax gave me an up-and-down look. "*You* are going into *the sewers*? Hard to believe it."

"Shut up." I rolled my eyes. "Let's go." I gave my friends one final hug before I headed out the back doors, with Jax following behind me.

"I don't think I much like being bossed around by a girl," he said as we made it into the alley.

I spun toward him with the royal flames in my eyes. "You don't have much of a choice. I told you a bargain with me would be serious. You made your bed, now lay in it!"

"Whoa, cool down, princess." He threw his hands up, palms facing out.

"Don't call me that! Especially in Irolyth. As a matter of fact, don't even call me Piper. No one can know who I am."

"And why is that? Wouldn't they be happy for their princess's return?"

"My family was hung before they could defend themselves against my uncle's words. I am not willing to take that chance. From here on out, call me..." I held my chin for a moment in contemplation. "Cami."

There was a long silent moment. A grave expression grew on his face. Jax took in a deep breath before he spoke. "Cami, it is. Just so you know, I am expecting a high reward for working with a future queen."

I rolled my eyes in response, then headed deeper into the alley. There were entrances to the sewers all over the city, but lucky for us, there was one in the alley near The White Rabbit. We were even luckier that there had been no rain in weeks. For that would make passage through the sewers unbearable. While they were dry, there were walkways, but if it had rained, they would be flooded.

Jax removed the grate, and I looked into the dark hole. The vile smell nearly knocked me off my feet. He motioned for me to go in first. The thin ladder felt as if it was going to collapse while I climbed down. Jax entered after me and covered the top with the grate.

As I hit the floor, I snapped my fingers, and three small fireballs appeared in the air around me, illuminating the sewers. Concrete pathways sat on either side of dark water.

"Well? Where to?" He asked as he put both feet on the ground and looked up and down the long length of the tunnel. Finally noticing the floating balls of fire, he stared at them in awe. He reached up to try to touch one.

I smacked his hand away from it before he could. "That is real fire. Careful not to get burned."

It had been years since I had passed through the sewers. I refused to come back, but I could not deny the pull I felt in my heart. The pull had always been there, calling me home. Guiding me to Irolyth.

"This way." I motioned. We came to a wide staircase leading to a large square room after about a ten-minute walk. On the far wall sat a portal, about seven feet tall and three feet wide. Red and yellow fog swirled and mixed within it. A shiver ran down my spine and traveled through my body. I had avoided this place since I passed through it all those years ago, and seeing it now, nearly brought me to my knees. The scent of sweet smoke filled the air, the scent of home.

Like a moth drawn to a flame, I walked directly to the portal and stopped in front of it, tears welled in my eyes. A firm hand gripped my shoulder, and I turned my head and looked into Jax's gaze.

"How long has it been?" He asked softly.

"Three years." I turned my head back to the portal. I was confused about why he was showing me this softer side of him. It was very different from the Jax I knew.

"Let's get you home." He stood by my side and took my hand. Heat rushed through my body as our fingers locked. I hated how right it felt to have his hand in mine.

After taking one more deep breath, we stepped into the portal together.

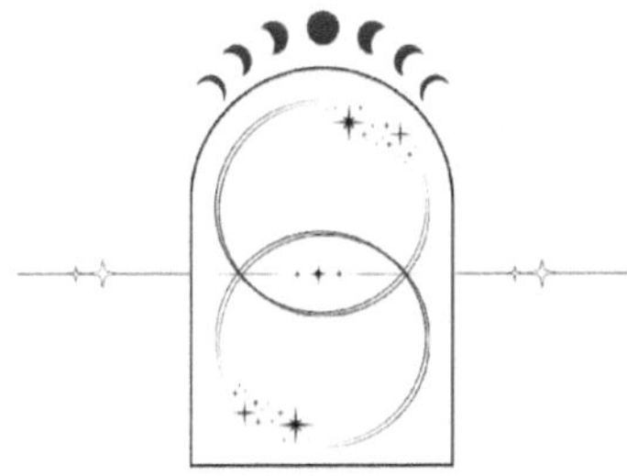

Seven

Once we were through the portal, I took a deep breath of the sweet air. Tears streamed down my face as I looked upon my homeland for the first time in three years. We stood on a small island surrounded by crimson water, and I fell to my knees and ran my hands against the scarlet grass. The sun beat down on me and warmed my skin. I'd nearly forgotten Jax was with me. It was his voice that caused me to look up.

"This place... is beautiful," he said in a hushed tone.

"This is the Sanguine Mire," I said as I stood. "Located in the southeast of Irolyth. Due to the terrain, it isn't a highly visited area."

"If I lived here, I would visit as often as I could. I've never seen anything like this."

Everything in Elswyth was dull. Color like this didn't exist there, at least not in the capital. He looked around and examined the new world around him. I had forgotten how large the redwood trees were that filled this land. The whole western and southern regions of Irolyth were taken over by the redwood forest. In the Mire, the trees grew out of the water, and they weren't as dense as other regions of the forest.

"Where to now... *Cami*?" He emphasized the name that I asked him to call me.

To be honest, I wasn't exactly sure. In my haste to trap Jax in the bargain, I failed to come up with a plan.

"You have no idea, do you?" He raised an eyebrow. "You have to be kidding me!" A deep chuckle escaped his throat.

"Sorry, I never expected to sneak back into my kingdom to reclaim my throne. I don't have some master plan!"

Jax crossed his arms and shook his head. "Well, first it would be wise to change your appearance, though you should have done that before we left Zamora."

"Change my appearance?"

"Well, you don't want people to know who you are." He ran his fingers through my hair.

Heat rose to my cheeks, and I found myself wishing he wouldn't drop his hand. For a moment, I thought I could grow to like this human. I quickly shoved those feelings down. He was right. Anyone who saw my red hair would know I was of royal blood. We were the only ones in Irolyth to have this color of hair. Inhaling deeply, my body tingled as magic ran through me.

Jax took a step back with the look of shock as I transformed. Now that I was home, I had full access to my magic. Back in Zamora, it felt as if it was only a small ember compared to the raging fire it should be. I heard rumors that across the ocean from Elswyth, there were several lands where fae roamed. I had always wanted to travel there to see if I would have a connection to my magic, but the King of Elswyth had banned travel to other continents.

While in Elswyth, I could only minimally change my appearance, just enough to make me appear human. Now, a totally different person stared back at Jax. I ran my fingers through my sleek, long black hair. My once green eyes were now a stormy gray to match his.

"Well... that's different," he said with an annoyed tone.

I smirked. "You don't like it?"

"No," he said in a cold voice, looking away. "It doesn't matter if I like it, anyway. Where is the closest town to here? We will need a place to stay. You wouldn't happen to have any money stashed nearby, would you? That would have been smart of you to do before you left."

"I was escaping death. Do you really think I had time to do that?"

"I suppose not." He rolled his eyes and walked over to the edge of the island. "Are you going to be okay walking through this, *Cami*?" Every time he called me that, venom dripped from his tongue.

"Northeast of here is a religious sanctuary called The Glade. They worship The Mother. We should travel there to seek refuge. Then we can figure out our next move."

Jax quickly picked me up and threw me over his shoulder. I squirmed in his arms, trying to get down. I was not used to being up this high. The more I struggled, the tighter Jax held onto me.

"Put me down!"

"I am not allowing you to walk in this water. I will carry you," he snapped.

I stopped fighting. "At least let me get on your back, so I'll be more comfortable."

"Fine." He put me down, and as soon as my feet hit the ground, he grabbed my chin and forced me to look up at him. My body trembled as he stepped closer, closing the gap between us. "I may be stuck in this bargain, and as soon as it is done, so are we. But I will protect you and take care of you while we are here. Do you understand me, *princess?*"

A chill ran down my spine as he said that last word. There was something about him calling me 'princess' that put me on edge. Especially since I told him not to do so. All I could do was nod in response.

"Good girl," he purred before turning around and kneeling.

Ignoring him, because I liked that way too much, I got onto his back. He looped his arms around my legs before standing. My body tensed as he held onto me tight and took his first step into the water. I wondered if I should tell him the water goes on for miles, or that it would take a whole day to get to The Glade.

He would find out on his own in good time.

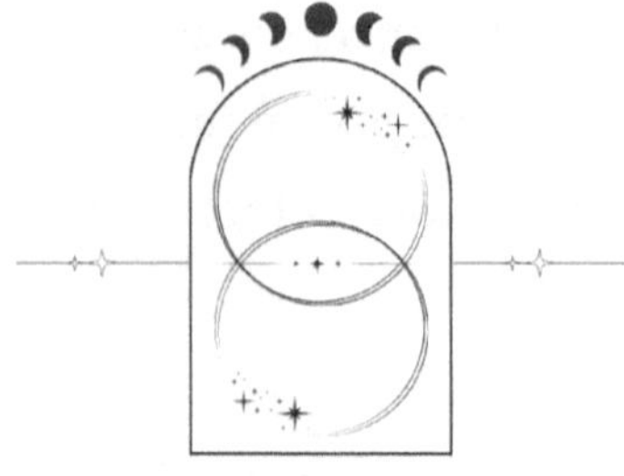

Eight

Several hours later, Jax dropped me onto the ground with a huff once we were out of the Mire and on dry land. His dark pants were soaking wet and clung to his body. We still had a long way to go before we reached The Glade. Jax began to take off his pants.

"Whoa, what are you doing?" I shouted at him as I held my hands up, motioning for him to stop.

"I am not walking around in soaking wet clothes. I need to let them dry before I put them back on," he said as his pants slid down to his knees.

"That is indecent! Put them back on!"

Jax grinned. "You know, you are the first girl to ever tell me that. Normally, girls like you beg me to remove them." He took a step closer to me.

Heat flooded my body and rose to my cheeks. I looked up to the sky, cursing myself for wanting to see more of him. Words jammed in my throat as he closed the gap between us.

"Too bad there isn't a pretty little firecracker who can dry them quickly for me."

"Don't call me that!" The words rushed out.

"Why not? I heard Steve and the owner of The White Rabbit call you that," he teased.

"Only my friends call me that." I shot him a pointed glare.

"Are we not friends, princess?" He winked, and that wicked smirk grew.

"No. We are not. Remember, you said once we are done here, then you will leave? Friends don't leave."

He chuckled. "Oh, you sweet little thing. There are many types of friendships. Ours is just situational. Now be a dear and dry my pants so we can hurry on." He shoved his pants into my hands and then looked around at the forest. "I've never seen trees like this before," he said as he raised his gaze toward the canopy. "I spent my whole life in Zamora. The only trees I've ever seen are the small ones that line the sidewalks."

Zamora was a concrete jungle. In the three years I lived there, I never saw a single park. Along some of the streets in the nicer parts of the city were small skinny trees. They bloomed little white flowers in the spring and caused the streets to be covered in petals and pollen.

"I suppose this is a huge change for you." Using my magic, heat ran through my body as I warmed the pants. The water quickly turned into steam, leaving the pants dry in little time. I tried hard not to look at his rear as he walked farther away from me, but this man was built like a god. "Here they are all dry." Taking a step forward, I extended them out to him.

He quickly took the pants from my hand and put them back on as he spoke. "What exactly can your magic do? Fire magic must come in handy often," he chuckled.

"Don't tell anyone about my fire magic," I blurted out.

"Why not?" He raised an eyebrow and cocked his head.

"Only the royal family has that power. We refer to it as the royal flames. The Mother gifted this to the Rossi family generations ago when we first ascended to the throne."

"Understood. If it was a gift from The Mother, shouldn't the people at this sanctuary be excited to see someone with one of her gifts?"

"I have no idea, but it's better not to test it."

"Which way to The Glade?" he asked. "We need to get moving. Walk and talk. Tell me about The Mother."

I pointed him in the right direction, and the two of us began our journey. "She is the creator of magic. Without her, the fae would be nothing more than elves."

"There are elves?" As we walked, his head kept moving, on the lookout for anything that may be coming at us.

"There were many years ago. The Mother blessed a small group of them with magic and created the fae. Long ago, there was a war between the elves and the fae. The fae prevailed, and the elves are long gone."

The forest was too silent. The only sound was our voices. It made me nervous as once this forest was crawling with life.

"That's dark."

"As is life." I shrugged. "Unfortunately, I learned the hard way, it is either kill or be killed. My father should have killed my uncle when they battled for the crown, but he spared him instead. In doing so, he caused his own death."

"They battled for the crown?"

"On their eighteenth birthday. They were twins, as are all royal siblings. When two males are born, they battle for the throne to the death. My father was the first to spare his brother. He said that ruling did not require bloodshed. Once he became king, he declared no longer brothers battle to the death. In sparing his brother, he condemned himself to the bloodshed he wanted to end." As I spoke, I increased my pace. I could not blame my father for sparing his brother. If I were male and my father did not change the laws, Alexander and I would have had to duel. I knew that I did not have the heart to kill my kin. When I lost my twin, I felt a part of me die inside. Did the other royal siblings feel this way after they murdered their twin, or was the thirst for power too great?

We continued to walk in silence. After a long moment, he spoke. "I'm sorry for your loss. I know how hard it is to lose a parent. My mother died when I was very young due to illness. I was at her bedside when she passed."

"I am so sorry. What about your father?"

"Never met him. My mother said he was a generous and kind man. But what man abandons the mother of his unborn child and leaves them to the streets?"

"No man at all," I responded.

"Exactly. Now, go back to The Mother," he said quickly, changing the subject. Jax brought his hand to his eyes, and I wondered if he thought I didn't see the silver mist in them.

I told him how The Mother granted six groups of fae different powers and provided them with their own place to reside. Long ago, all the fae realms were one, but it only caused chaos once our magics were awoken. The Mother separated the realms, to keep us from killing each other. The fae of Irolyth had fire and forest magic. Orilon had control over the shadows. Aeros had gravitational magic, and thank The Mother for it, as they needed it to escape The Great Calamity. The shifters of Khaldon lived inside a mountain. Alari was the territory of the water fae. The final fae realm was Tarak, but little was known about this realm. To my knowledge, a portal to them had not been found. They had completely isolated themselves.

Not only was The Mother the giver of magic, but she also was the mother to all of our gods. She gave away pieces of herself to create her children. Each with their own gifts. I remember sitting in church each week and staring at the stained glass that depicted all the gods, and I was always drawn to Aurora, the goddess of Flames and Light. A beautiful red-haired goddess with fire in her eyes. It was said she was the first to carry the royal flames and the Rossi line were her descendants.

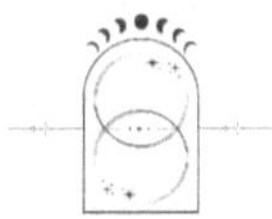

Hours into our walk, an arrow whizzed between our heads and struck the tree behind us. A woman in a white hooded robe stepped out from behind a tree with another arrow ready. Her golden hair was in two braids that ran down her front to her waist, and the silver and ruby circlet around her head told me exactly which group this woman belonged to.

"Who are you?" She asked.

Before I answered, I fell to my knees and bowed my head. Jax immediately followed my lead. "Lady of the Flame, we come seeking refuge. We have traveled far to find The Glade and rest under The Mother's protection. My name is Cami, and this is my mate, Jax." My skin crawled at calling someone like Jax my mate. He was so rude and arrogant. I hated to admit he was also extremely handsome and charming.

The Lady of the Flame lowered her bow and rushed over to us. "Are you from Mayrin? I fear the situation there has gotten worse."

My gaze shot up to meet her as fear ran through my body. Mayrin was the capital city that was just south of the castle. I spent many of my days there as a child, shopping and speaking with the locals. My father always taught me even though we were royalty, we were not better than the common man. We were all blessed by The Mother, and we should treat everyone justly.

"We are. We could not stay any longer," Jax said.

"Please rise. We will get you settled right away." She took my hand. Accepting her assistance, I stood. Jax followed suit as well, and we allowed her to guide us to The Glade. We stepped through some short and dense trees and the leaf-covered ground turned into pale stone. The Lady of the Flame waved her hand in the air, and the temple was revealed to us. It was just as beautiful as I remembered. The white marble was covered in crawling red ivy. The center structure was two stories high, the first floor was for worship, and the top housed the Ladies of the Flame. Three smaller buildings surrounded the temple. One was a library, one was housing, and the third was a well-kept secret.

"King Joffrey is ruining this land. We should have never trusted him. May The Mother forgive us for what we allowed to happen to King Klaus, Queen Cassia, and Crown Prince Alexander. Let us pray Princess Piper returns to save us."

My heart dropped.

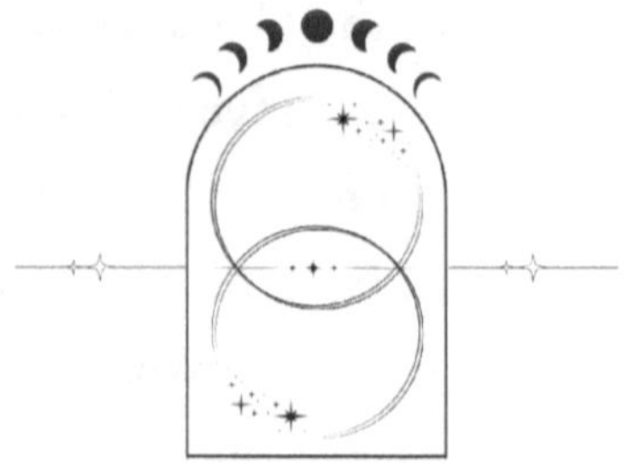

Nine

"Do you think the princess is still out there?" I asked, not wanting to reveal myself.

She offered me a soft smile. "The Mother keeps her safe. I know she is protected."

She guided us into the center building, where three other robed women stood near the entryway, all with the silver circlet in their hair. They turned toward us as we entered. I noticed the pews of the worship hall were full of people not in robes. There were several Ladies of the Flame passing out food, clothing, and other items to the congregation. My stomach turned. Were these all people from Mayrin?

"Lady Stella," one of them said to the woman guiding us. The red trim of her robe indicated she was the Head

Lady. Nothing in this place happened without her approval.

"Lady Rae, I found two more refugees out in the forest. They are also from Mayrin."

The three rushed over to us. "You poor dears. We are at capacity, so I don't know if we will be able to take anyone else in," the woman with the red-trimmed robe said.

One of the Ladies stared at Jax with an intense glare. She stepped closer to him, reached up, and touched his rounded ears. In my haste to glamour myself to make sure people could not recognize me, I'd forgotten to glamour him to look fae.

"What strange ears," she whispered.

The other woman grabbed his arm and examined his tattoos. I couldn't help the anger surging through me. I hated that they were touching him.

"And strange tattoos." The second one added.

The third woman turned her attention from Lady Stella to Jax. She slowly gave him an up-and-down look, and the grin on her face grew. "Are you from Orilon? It has been a long time since we have seen a fae from there."

"He is," I said quickly. "He lost his powers due to the curse and left before he could turn into one of those horrid creatures. The Mother protects him here." It felt so wrong lying in a place like this, but I had to if we wanted to stay safe.

"How sad." The girl who was touching his ear was now running her hands through his hair.

He had the stupidest grin on his face as the Ladies fawned over him. He even was playing with one's golden locks.

With her hands still on Jax's arms, she looked over to Lady Rae with big doe eyes. "We have to let them stay. We can't abandon them."

Lady Rae took a deep breath and glanced at Lady Stella. "Prepare them for the unveiling. If they pass. They can stay."

"The unveiling?" I asked.

"Joffrey has sent in glamoured spies in the past. The unveiling will remove any glamour you may have and reveal your true form," Lady Stella said.

A lump formed in my throat. Jax pulled away from the women, came to my side, and took my hand, giving it a gentle squeeze. Calmness washed over me when he offered me a soft smile. Something about the assassin brought me comfort, even when I first gazed into his storm gray eyes and Steve had told me to stay away.

"We would expect nothing less," he chimed. "You must keep The Glade safe."

"Lady Stella," Lady Rae said, "Please take them to the inner sanctum and prepare them for the ceremony."

"Yes, my lady," she answered with a bow. Gesturing for the two of us to follow her. "Come along."

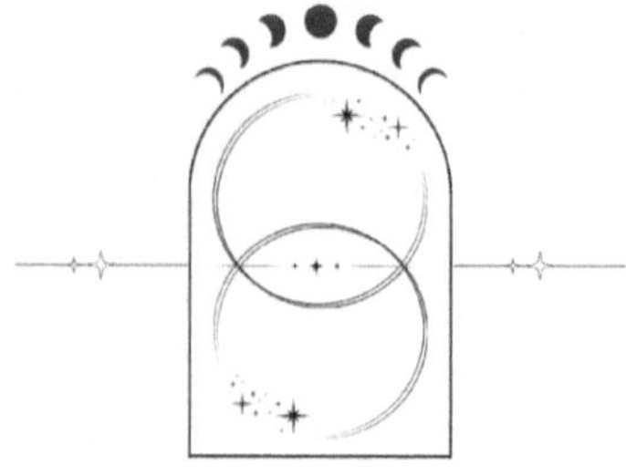

Ten

Stella guided us to the back of the temple and down a flight of stairs. As we walked, the torches lit when we neared and extinguished as we passed. My stomach twisted, and I felt I was going to fall with each step. Jax looked cool and collected, and I wish I knew what was going through his head. There was no way I could go through with this ritual. The unveiling would be disastrous.

Or would it?

They seemed to hate my uncle and saw him for the monster he truly was. If I revealed myself, would they help me? Would they be mad at for us deceiving them? Would they be what Jax and I needed to succeed in our mission? I couldn't deny I made a huge mistake in not thinking anything through before I trapped a human assassin in this deal and returned to Irolyth.

At the bottom of the stairs was a single square room made of stone. In its center was a pool of aquamarine glittering water. Steam gently rose above the water. Near the far wall, two tall, unlit red candles sat on each end of the altar. Behind it was a large golden statue of The Mother. I could feel her gaze on me, and a shiver ran down my spine.

It was then I knew I needed to tell the truth.

"Lady Stella," I whispered, my voice shaking.

She turned to me with concern on her face. "Yes?"

"Can you please bring Lady Rae down here? Just you and her. It is urgent."

Stella's eyes went wide, and she nodded. "Of course." Before anyone could say anything else, she was already ascending the stairs.

Jax grabbed me by my arm and pulled me close. "What are you doing?" He grumbled.

"We were not going to make it through the unveiling without them finding out. It's best to come clean."

"I had a plan! You do not have to tell them who you are! You stupid girl. You are going to ruin this." Anger built in his voice.

I wanted to cower as he spoke, but I held my head high and kept his gaze. "What plan? How were you going to get past the unveiling and keep my identity a secret with no magic?" My heart sank as I saw what was in his other hand. An unsheathed blade. I shouldn't have been surprised, but a part of me was. It is to be expected an assassin would resort to such things when backed into a corner. "Put that away. No one is dying today," I said in a low and serious tone.

He released me, and his lips quirked as he sheathed his blade. "You surprise me, princess. Anyone else would show fear when held tight by me with a blade."

"I escaped death once already. I am not afraid. Death excites me." I teased.

Lady Rae returned with Lady Stella and both of them held concerned looks. Rae stopped in front of me and lowered her gaze to meet mine.

"Lady Stella said you had urgent news for us?" She asked with a tone of annoyance.

"I do," I whispered, praying to The Mother I was making the right choice. "It's about the lost princess."

"What do you know?" She demanded.

Taking a deep, steadying breath, I removed my glamour and watched as Stella and Rae looked at me in shock. "I am Princess Piper Camilla Rossi."

Lady Stella fell to her knees and bowed her head. "Princess, welcome home."

Rae gave me a judgmental glare that would have burned through me if she had the royal flames. "How can we be so sure this is not a ruse?"

"I understand your worry, but it's not. I am sorry I misled you. I just returned to Irolyth, and I was afraid of what I was returning to. I did not expect a world where I would be wanted. I expected the first person to see me to call the guards and demand I be hung like my family. I will complete the unveiling and show you what I am saying to be true."

"I cannot blame you for being afraid. What King Joffrey has put you through, I could not even imagine. Please, step into the waters of truth. Unveil yourself to us," Lady Rae said.

As I stepped toward the water, Jax gently touched my hand, pulling me to him. "You're lucky this went in your favor, but next time, don't do anything without consulting me first," he whispered, then released me.

I didn't respond and walked to the pool. When I stepped into the warm water, my flames came alive within me. The two candles on the altar lit as I walked toward the center of the pool.

"Please, fully submerge yourself," Lady Rae said. All three stood at the water's edge with awaiting gazes. My eyes locked onto Rae's as I dunked myself underwater. Warmth flooded me. When I surfaced, I pushed away the hair that clung to my face.

"Princess," Lady Rae said humbly as she knelt. "I apologize. After all this time, I needed to take precautions. Stella, fetch the princess a towel."

Stella rushed and grabbed a white towel off the rock, then returned to the pool's edge. As I stepped out, she wrapped the towel around me. I took in a deep inhale. The towel smelt like roses. Tears welled my eyes, reminding me of my mother. Before she wed my father, she was a Lady of the Flame. She told me she used to tend to a rose garden here. It reminded her of her sisters, who were all named after flowers. That is where she met my father for the first time. Rae's voice pulled me from my memories.

"Well, man from Orilon, are you who you claim to be?"

He chuckled. "Not at all. I am a human from Elswyth. Trapped by duty to serve."

"Trapped by duty?" The Ladies asked in unison.

It was then I informed them all that had happened these last three years. Including how I tricked a human assassin into helping me on my journey.

"Well, human," Rae said in a stern voice, "step into the pool. Unveil yourself."

With a grumble, Jax did as she said. "I hate getting wet. This is going to mess up my hair."

When he got to the center, he turned back toward us, and his stormy gray eyes were glued to mine. He took a deep breath and dunked himself underwater. The candles on the altar went out, and the room fell into darkness. The sparkling blue water was now a black abyss.

When Jax emerged, his eyes were as dark and endless as the void he stood in.

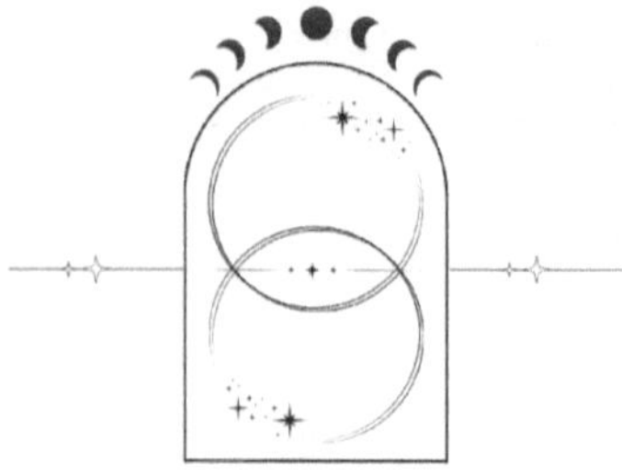

Eleven

The ladies grabbed my arms and pulled me away from the pool in a panic. I couldn't pull my gaze from Jax. His dark hair stuck to his skin, and water dripped down his body. His shirt clung to him and showed off his muscles. Looking into his darkened eyes, I knew I should be afraid. Instead, I found comfort.

"Mother save us," Stella whispered.

"Impossible," Rae said. She released my arm and stepped forward. "Begone foul beast!"

Jax turned his gaze on her. "I am no foul beast." His voice was darker and deeper compared to his normal tone.

"There are many legends of The Shadow coming to snuff out the royal flame. Begone. You are not welcome here!" Rae said in a louder tone.

My heart dropped. I had heard whispers of The Shadow. Many believed it to be the symbol of the end of times. Did Jax know who I was before I even approached him?

"Jax, when you went underwater, all the lights went out, and the water turned black. And your eyes..." I started but trailed off.

I went to take a step forward, but Rae held up her arm to block my path. "Princess, stay back!"

"No, let me go to him!" I tried to move past her, but Stella pulled me back.

"Princess, it is not safe!"

"Do not touch her!" Jax roared.

I watched as he vanished into the darkness. A feeling of unease took over me. I looked around the room frantically for any sign of Jax.

"We must go! Now!" Rae's voice shook as she grabbed my wrist and pulled me toward the exit.

I tried to yank away as I looked back at the now-empty pool. The water had returned to the shimmering aquamarine shade it had been earlier. Stella's scream startled us all. We had almost made it to the stairs, and Jax stood directly in front of us, blocking our way.

Water dripped from his body, and his shadow tattoos looked like they were moving as if they had come to life. Rae put me behind her and Stella. She looked over her shoulder, and it was terror I saw in her hazel eyes.

"I said release her," Jax said in a low growl.

"We won't let you harm the princess. She will reclaim her throne, become queen of this land, and the royal flames will rid the darkness. Irolyth will be no place for you, Shadow!"

"Hurt her? I would never hurt her." Rage filled his eyes and his nostrils flared. "I will help her claim her throne. I will rid the world of the man that hurt her." On that last word, he vanished once again.

Rae and Stella looked around in confusion. A chill shot through me, and when I went to turn my head, something inside me wouldn't allow me to. An arm wrapped around my waist and pulled me back into something firm and wet.

"Every flame casts a shadow. I fully intend on being yours, princess," Jax purred in my ear. My body finally allowed me to move, and I turned my head to see him gazing down at me with a smirk. He looked at the Ladies while holding me close. "I will protect her with my life. The only flame I plan to snuff out is Joffrey's. However, if you try to keep her away from me again, I will destroy this entire sanctuary. Do you understand?" He growled.

"How do we know you are telling the truth?" Rae asked.

"You don't. I do not blame you for the stories that have twisted my name. But, know this to be fact. If you intend on even trying to take her, you will suffer. Everyone here will suffer. She is mine. I am hers. The Mother created me for Piper. Will you go against your Mother's will?"

Something inside of me knew what he said to be the truth. When I gently pressed into him, his grip on me loosened slightly.

Rae and Stella just stared at him for a moment before they agreed. Rae took a step forward, hesitating before speaking. "We will trust you, for now. But if you do anything to harm her, you will meet your end. Come along, and let me take you to your chambers."

Jax released me and came to my side. He took my hand in his and smiled down at me. His eyes were now back to the stormy gray I was familiar with, and his tattoos were now static on his body. "I think that sounds wonderful. Our princess needs her rest after the journey we've had."

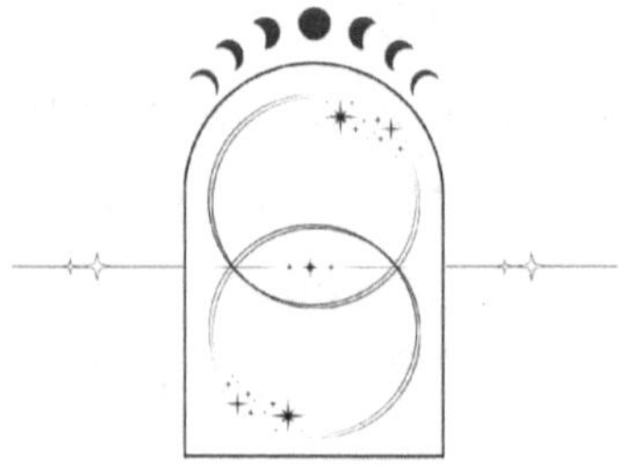

Twelve

Stella and Rae took us to the building behind the main building of the sanctuary that I had never been in before. The entry floor was a large room with beautiful white marble columns that matched the floor. The walls were painted a light tangerine. Two staircases led to a floor above and one below. A fire danced within the hearth in the center of the room.

"Up the stairs will be your living quarters while you're here," Rae said. "Downstairs is off limits for now. If you need anything, all you need to do is ask."

With that, Stella and Rae gave their goodbyes, not looking at Jax as they left. The two of us went upstairs and opened the door to our living quarters. It was truly magnificent. There was a large sitting room decorated exactly how my parents decorated their royal apartments. The furniture was upholstered with deep orange velvet with gold accents. I smiled as I admired the painting of the redwood forest in autumn hung above the fireplace. To the right was a fully stocked kitchen. My stomach growled as I thought of food. It had been way too long since I last ate. On the left side of the sitting room was a staircase that led to an open hallway. The railing was twisted golden bars.

There was a single door in the center of the hall made of stained glass in the image of flames. We entered the room and found a beautifully furnished bedroom. One large bed sat in the center against the back wall, with a dark orange covering that matched the furniture downstairs. There was a closet on the left wall full of clothes that the Ladies said we could help ourselves to. To the right were double frosted glass doors that led to a bathroom.

Jax and I hadn't spoken since leaving the unveiling. There was so much I wanted to ask, so much I needed to say. But it was he who broke the silence.

"I will wait outside while you change into dry clothes." He left and shut the stained-glass door behind him before I could respond.

I went into the bathroom and peeled off my soaking wet clothes. The towel they provided after the ritual did very little to dry me; I was still soaking wet.

I quickly took a shower, dried off, and got dressed. When I returned downstairs, Jax was sitting on the floor cross-legged in front of the fireplace, intensely staring at the flames. I walked over to his side and lowered my gaze, curious if he would say anything before I did. His stormy gray eyes looked up at me.

"Did you know what you are?" Were the only words I could get to leave my lips.

"Not until the unveiling. When I was underwater, everything was revealed to me by The Mother. I swear I didn't know who you were or what I was when I walked into The White Rabbit. I only went there to bother Steve."

Taking a deep breath, I sat down on the floor next to him. "What exactly did you see?"

He let out a low chuckle. "I saw inside me lies a shadow spirit, originally from the realm of Orilon. It entered my body the moment I was born. It had been with me all along. There had been moments in my life where my powers manifested without me even knowing. The Mother showed me the truth behind those moments that I assumed were just luck. These powers have allowed me to become the best assassin in Elswyth." He turned his gaze back to the fire. "I saw it is my duty to serve you, even beyond our deal. That I am to do the hard things you cannot. That I am to be your sword and shield. That I am to help you become queen."

I leaned my head against his shoulder, and he wrapped his arm around me, pulling me in close. His touch filled me with comfort. "I'm scared," I whispered.

"Of?"

"Being queen. It was never my path. My brother was to be king, so I spent my entire life learning my place was to serve the crown. To be wed for political gain. Never to be more than a trophy."

Jax gently took my chin in his hand and forced me to look into his eyes. "You are no trophy. You are not a pawn for political gain. You will make a powerful and fair queen. It will be an honor to serve you." He leaned down and gently pressed his lips to mine.

Frozen in shock, heat rushed through my body. I saw the fire flare out of the corner of my eye. Finally, I made my move. Wrapping my arms around his neck, I pressed into him.

He pulled away and gave me a soft smile. "Gods, I have been wanting to do that since we sealed the bargain." He stood and walked toward the stairs. "As much as I'd like to stay and do that some more, I need to go take a shower. Tonight we will rest. Tomorrow we will worry about the weight of the world."

I watched him walk up the stairs until he rounded the corner out of sight. Did that really just happen? Did he really just kiss me? I sat there for a while in silence, staring into the flames just as he had been earlier.

After some time, my stomach let out a loud growl, and I entered the kitchen. We hadn't eaten since leaving Elswyth. I decided while Jax was in the shower, I would prepare our meal. Opening the fridge, I perused the ingredients. Two steaks, an onion, butter, cream, stock, a dry white wine, pasta, and seasonings were exactly what I needed.

With everything ready, the idea of the meal formed, and I got to work. I loved to cook, but it was my mother who instilled her love of cooking in me. Every Sunday, she gave the kitchen staff the day off. We would prepare the meals for the family. My love of cooking was the only thing I took to Elswyth as a reminder of my family. This meal was the first one I'd made for Steph when she took me in.

I missed her and Steve more than I could imagine, I wasn't sure if or when I would see them again. The White Rabbit had been my home, and the people there had quickly become my family when I thought I was alone in the world. When everything in Irolyth was said and done, I hoped I could return to show how much they meant to me. Part of me wondered if Steph knew Jax had a shadow spirit in him. She rarely used her magic in my presence, so I was unaware of how powerful she was.

She said her mother and aunt had used it to do terrible things. That magic in Elswyth corrupted the good within people. Power had turned them into monsters.

"It smells good in here." Jax's voice pulled me out of my thoughts.

I almost dropped the wooden spoon I was holding. He stood in the doorway with only a towel wrapped around his waist. His dark hair was slicked back, and beads of water dripped down his muscles. Heat flooded my body at the sight, and I could not help to wish he dropped the towel. I quickly returned my gaze to the onions caramelizing in the pan.

"Thank you. It's going to taste just as good." My body tensed as Jax came over and stood directly behind me. He reached around me and took the spoon out of my hand. My gaze followed the spoon as he brought it to his lips.

"You're right," he purred after he took a taste.

"Why don't you go get dressed so I can finish cooking?" I forced the words to pass my lips. To be honest, I wanted nothing more than for him to drop the towel right here.

"Is that truly what you want, princess?" Longing flashed through those gray eyes.

I turned to face him, swallowing hard as I met his gaze. "You're distracting me, and if I burn this meal, I will be very upset."

A predatory grin grew on his face. "Kiss me, and I will go get dressed."

"You already stole one kiss. Do you think you deserve another?" My entire body tingled. I couldn't believe the conversation we were having.

"Absolutely not. However, that hasn't stopped you from enjoying my kisses. I will steal another, and later, after dinner, you're going to be begging for a lot more than just kisses." Before I could respond, his lips were on mine once again. This time, they were passionate and hungry.

I leaned into his kiss and matched his fire. Wrapping my arms around his neck, I pressed my body into his. Our tongues danced with each other, and I found myself craving more. When he pulled away, I wished he hadn't.

"I-I should get back to cooking."

"I will go get dressed now, princess. I can't wait to eat. I'm starving." He slowly gave me an up-and-down glance, slowly licking his top lip. With a wink, he pulled away from me, exited the room, and walked upstairs.

I couldn't help but watch him until he vanished into the shadows, just as he did in the ritual chamber. Part of me hoped he would have sat me on the kitchen counter and taken me right here.

Quickly, I stuffed down those feelings. I turned my attention back on cooking and put all of my frustrations into making this the best dish I had ever made.

About thirty minutes later, I had the table set with two delicious plates of creamy caramelized onion pasta, topped with a sliced steak seasoned with fresh herbs. Jax returned downstairs in a loose black top and gray pants just as I had finished plating,

He inhaled deeply and a smile grew on his face. "Thank you for making this. I can't wait to eat," he said as he sat down at the table.

I sat next to him and offered a smile. "I hope you like it."

"I like you. So, I like anything you make." He picked up his fork and began eating.

Heat flooded my cheeks once again at the compliment. I didn't even know how to respond. Before Joffrey's betrayal, I did not have any men courting me. At The White Rabbit, the only men interested in me were extremely wasted. I never thought I would be in The Glade sitting at a table with a man I was smitten with.

"Eat," he said with his fork held up to my mouth. It had a swirl of pasta and a small piece of steak. I opened my mouth, and he gently slid it in. The flavors burst on my tongue, and I melted in delight.

I truly outdid myself with this meal. It was perfect.

"Now eat your own. You owe me a bite." He pulled his fork from my mouth and immediately took a swirl of pasta off of my plate and put it into his own mouth. "It's too good not to get as much as I can," he chuckled.

"Hey! You chose to give me some of yours. That's on you." I readied another bite on my fork.

"You got me there."

"I think now that we have a safe house, we need to start a plan on what to do next."

"Tomorrow, princess. We will worry about all that tomorrow. Rest."

"But—"

"Shh." He put another bite of pasta into my mouth. "Eat. Rest. I will clean up the kitchen after we are done eating."

The two of us dined together, and I found myself excited to be in his company. Once we were done eating, Jax cleaned up the kitchen just as he'd said. I went upstairs into the bedroom, and with a snap of my fingers, the fireplace ignited. I fell into bed and took a deep breath. The softness of the mattress reminded me of the luxury back at the castle. Gods, how I had missed it. For the first time in a while, I closed my eyes and allowed myself to relax.

After a few moments, Jax's voice broke the silence. "Are you ready to go to sleep, princess?"

I opened my eyes and sat up, yawning. "I think so. I'm exhausted."

He strode into the room and stopped just in front of me. "What side of the bed do you want?"

It was then it finally dawned on me there was only one bed. Did he expect to share it with me? "I plan on sleeping in the middle. You are sleeping downstairs."

He threw his head back and laughed. "No. I am sleeping in this bed. With you. I do not trust you being alone."

"What do you mean, you don't trust me?" I stood and furrowed my brow.

"I trust you. What I don't trust is this place, these people. I will give you five minutes to get into your night clothes." He winked, turned, and left the room.

All I could do was stare at the door. Never had I shared my bed with a man. My heart raced at the idea of him being so close to me. As much as I wanted to hate the arrogant assassin, I could not stop myself from falling for him. But there was no time for that now, not with everything that was on the line. I went over to the closet and picked out a red silky set. It was the only one that came with pants. The others were tiny slips that would reveal way too much. I nearly jumped out of my skin as I heard Jax's voice from behind me just as I finished changing.

"Damn, I am too late for the show. What a shame."

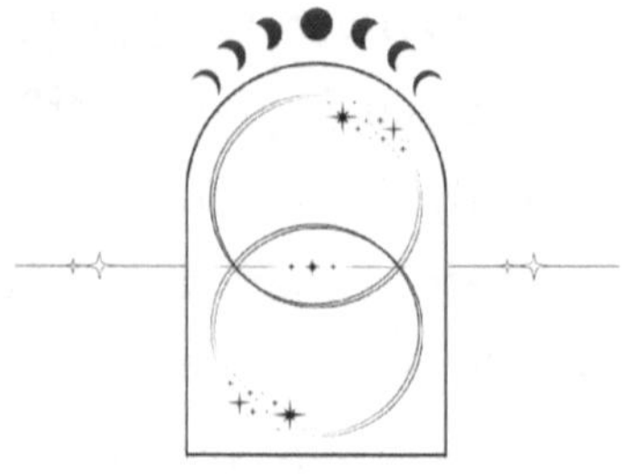

Thirteen

My heart pounded in my chest. Jax leaned against the door frame, shirtless. Heat rose to my cheeks as I met his predatory stare and he closed the space between us. Quickly, I looked away, but he placed his thumb under my chin and lifted my head, forcing me to meet his gaze.

"Do you like what you see, princess?" A delicate purr escaped his lips.

Words jammed in my throat as I tried to form a coherent response. After a moment of stuttering, I was finally able to speak. "It's time for bed. I am going to put pillows down the center. You will have your side, and I will have mine."

He let out a deep chuckle. "You think if I wanted to take you, those pillows would stop me from doing so?"

My body tensed at his words. But I couldn't help being intrigued. I hated that I couldn't get the image of his hands exploring my body out of my mind. His touch was now all I craved. Quickly, I forced down those feelings. There was no room for romance at a time like this. My main focus needed to be reclaiming my throne. I cannot allow myself to be distracted.

It was hard to tell if these feelings were real, or if they were just due to heightened emotions.

Stepping away from him, I shot him a pointed glare. "Good night, Jax."

The cocky grin on his face dropped. "Good night," he grumbled.

The two of us got into bed. Wanting to keep the most distance between us as I could, I clung to the edge. I snapped my fingers, and the fire dimmed so it could keep us warm, but the light wouldn't keep us awake. It seemed like I laid there for hours, my body refusing to give into sleep's sweet embrace. My mind kept racing and debating over matters of duty and heart.

I rolled over and saw Jax staring up at the ceiling. He looked over at me and broke the silence. "I didn't mean to upset you."

"You didn't. I just need to focus on the path ahead. The weight of saving my kingdom is too heavy to let myself worry about anything else," I said.

Jax scooted closer to me and smiled. "Well, I'm glad I didn't upset you. As for your burdens, let me help carry them. You are not alone in this. I am here by your side and will help you burn down the world if that's what it takes."

I offered him a soft smile and moved closer to the center of the bed. "The Fire Queen needs her Shadow."

"The Shadow is nothing without his Fire Queen," he responded.

On that last word, the two of us sat up and crashed our lips together. The fire across the room roared in response as I wrapped my arms around his neck and slid my fingers through his dark hair. Jax grabbed me by the waist and pulled me to sit on top of him. His kiss turned rough as he held me close. After a time that felt too short, our lips parted.

"Praise The Mother," I whispered.

"The only goddess I wish to worship is you."

His lips were back on mine, and I craved more. I cursed myself for the nightclothes I'd chosen, now wishing I'd picked something that would have given him better access to my body. I quickly pulled my top off and revealed to him my bare breasts.

"Beautiful," he groaned as he leaned down and took one of my nipples into his mouth. As he gently sucked on it, his hand found its way to my other breast, and he rolled my nipple in between his middle finger and thumb.

A moan escaped my lips. Grinding on his lap, I made small circles with my hips, and he thrusted up against me. There was nothing I wanted more than to feel him deep inside me. For the first time, I found a man who I wanted to give myself fully to. Ecstasy ran through my body as he grazed his teeth over my nipple. When he looked up at me with those stormy eyes, I nearly melted.

"Take those pants off before I rip them off of you to expose that beautiful little cunt of yours," he growled.

I quickly did as he commanded, and he did the same, unveiling his considerable length. Never did I imagine that it would be that large. It was hard to imagine that it could fit inside of me. The girth of it had my body quivering at the sight alone. Jax pulled me on top of him once again, quickly lining himself up with my entrance. He wasted no time slowly lowering me onto him. My eyes rolled back as I felt myself stretch to be able to take him. When he was as deep as he could go, I moved my hips in circular motions.

Jax let out a groan as he started thrusting into me, in and out, with no mercy. I placed my hands on his chest for support as he pounded into me, moaning to the rhythm of him.

"You feel as if you were made for me," he moaned. A moment later, he stopped thrusting. "Bounce on my cock," he demanded.

"It was you that was made for me," I purred in response. I obliged his command and gradually increased my pace until I was slamming myself down onto him. Jax held onto my hips tightly as I rode him. Mother, he was perfect. I would give up almost anything to stay in this moment for all eternity.

Without warning, Jax flipped us over so I was on my back. He began his merciless thrusts once again. Arching my back, I screamed his name. Stars filled my vision as I found my pleasure. He slowed down but continued hitting the deepest part of me. An eruption of heat filled my core, and Jax let out a roar as he pushed deep into me and held himself there as his release filled me.

He leaned down and planted his lips on mine. Breaking up the kiss, he growled, "Mine." When he pulled out of me, his essence spilled out. An emptiness took over me, and I found myself craving him once again. Jax reached down and, with two fingers, stroked me while gathering what had fallen out. He then gently pushed it back inside.

"Don't you dare waste a single drop," he growled.

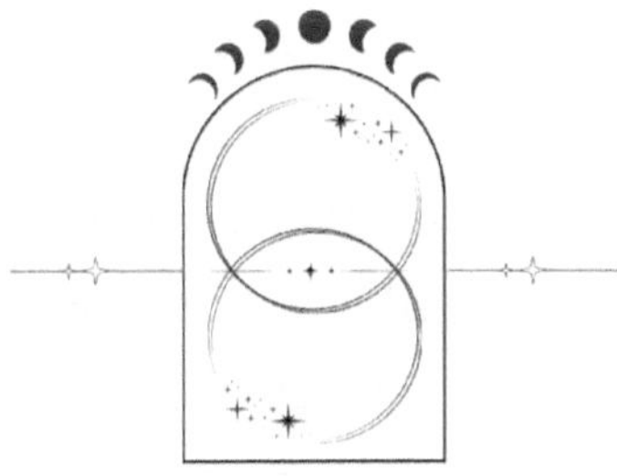

Fourteen

The next morning, I awoke in Jax's arms. The fire still blazed across the room, sending heat through my body. I snuggled my head into his chest, and my thoughts started to spiral. After everything was said and done, what would be next for us? Would he return to Elswyth, or would he stay here with me?

He gently ran his fingers through my hair. I lifted my head and saw him smiling down at me with sleep still in his eyes. He looked so calm, I wished we could stay locked in this moment for eternity. With a yawn, he held me tight against him.

"I never want to leave this bed," he purred.

"Then let's not. At least, not right now." I planted a kiss on his soft and tender lips.

A moment later, a knock sounded on the door leading out of the suite. Jax let out a growl and got out of bed, quickly put on his pants, and left the bedroom. I wrapped a robe around myself and went over to the bedroom door. I peeked out and over the balcony to see he was already downstairs and the door was open. Rae and Stella both stood just outside.

"Good morning," Rae said with venom in her words. She gave him a pointed up-and-down glare, then forced herself past him as she walked in. Stella followed in behind her.

"Why yes, please come in," Jax said, rolling his eyes.

"Where is the princess? What have you done to her?" Rae spat.

I made my way over to the railing and looked down at the three of them. "I'm here. Please give me a moment to get ready and I will be right down."

The Ladies' eyes went wide when their attention landed on me. I'm sure they knew exactly what had happened last night between Jax and me based on the way we were both dressed. Before they could say anything, I turned and walked into the bedroom. Once my clothes for the day were selected and laid on the bed, I entered the bathroom to finish getting ready.

When I was all ready for the day, I took a look in the mirror. I wore an orange and gold top with long bell sleeves and black pants. I put my wavy hair into a top bun with a few pieces left out to frame my face. When I looked into my green eyes, it took everything in me not to cry. The person I saw reflecting back wasn't me.

It was my mother.

I prayed to The Mother I would be half the queen she was. Cassia Regina Rossi was one of the most beloved queens in all of Irolyth's history. Until my uncle's lies had our people turning on us. To my mother, serving the crown meant serving the people. She wanted what was best for all, not just those who were high-born.

She came from a line of fae that had great powers gifted by nature itself. She and her sisters were all named after flowers. I never met any of them, they were all spread through the fae realms. My grandmother was one of the only fae from Tarak to leave the realm to travel to all of the realms. Unfortunately, she was never able to return to Tarak. She passed away long before I was born. My mother told me many stories about her family and how kind they were. Without my mother's magic and teachings, the farms of Irolyth would not be as successful as they are today.

As I descended the stairs, all eyes were on me. Stella and Jax both sat on the couch, and Rae was standing at the bottom landing.

"Princess Piper," she began with a deep breath, "We understand the next part of your journey is long. We understand what road you must travel down to free the people of Irolyth. However, before you can travel down that path, there is one more thing you must do."

"What is that?"

"You must speak to The Mother. You must get her approval to rule. Your father did the same before he ascended the throne, and so did all who came before him. Joffrey did not. He spat in the face of our most sacred traditions."

I raised an eyebrow. "Speak to The Mother?"

Rae hooked her arm around my elbow. "Yes, come. All will become clear in time."

Jax jumped from his seat. "Great. Where are we going?"

"You will be staying here with me," Lady Stella said.

"No. I go where she goes."

Rae shot him a glare. "Do you, too, spit in our faces? Will you also throw away our rituals and traditions, Shadow?"

Jax let out a low snarl and looked over to me. I gave him a small nod, and he sat back in his seat. "Fine. How long will this take?"

"Not long. Only an hour or so," Rae answered without a care.

"If she is not back in two hours, I will destroy this entire place to get to her."

"No need for all that. She will return shortly," Lady Stella assured him.

Rae turned her attention toward me. "Come along now, princess."

She guided me to the room where the unveiling had taken place. My heart pounded in my chest as I relived what had happened yesterday. We walked around the pool and stopped before the effigy of the Mother. On the altar in front of it was a golden bowl with some herbs and salts, surrounded by white candles.

I looked up at the golden statue and took a deep breath. Rae walked around to the other side of the altar and extended her hand.

"Please trust me. Please give me your hand, palm up," she said in a soft voice.

I gave her my hand, and she held it tightly. An athame blade magically appeared in her hand, and she quickly ran it over my palm, causing blood to pool in my hand. She turned my hand, and the blood spilled into the bowl. The candles ignited one by one, and when the last one sparked to life, everything faded to black.

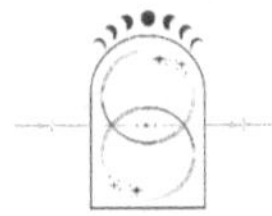

I awoke, standing in a marble room with pillars lining the walls. I spun around to see there were no doors or windows. My heart pounded in my chest, and my breathing became quick and shallow.

"Calm now, little flame," a soothing and feminine voice said.

My attention snapped to the far end of the room where The Mother sat on a marble throne in a long, white tulle gown. Her blonde hair fell in loose waves around her. Our gazes met, and calmness washed over me. She stood and stepped down from the dais.

"Where... Where am I?" I asked.

"You are in a part of my home. I closed off the rest to you. We would not wish for you to get lost in these eternal halls." In a blink, she was directly before me. She took my hands in hers and smiled. "Tell me why you are here, little flame."

"I need your blessing," I said meekly. Before The Mother, I was no one. How dare I ask her for anything? I should be grateful to bask in her ethereal glow.

"My blessing?" She raised a brow.

"I wish to become Queen of Irolyth," I said, forcing out every drop of confidence I had.

"Why now? Why not three years ago? Why not three years from now?"

"I am ready now. When I ran, I was a coward. I did not realize what I was leaving my people to." I dropped to my knees and lowered my head. "Please, allow me to save them."

She let out a soft hum. "Everything has happened just as it should have." My gaze snapped up with wide eyes. "You were not ready to reign at sixteen. You needed to find yourself. You needed to find him." She gently pulled me up to my feet.

"Jax?"

She nodded. "I spread rumors of The Shadow being a monster to destroy the kingdom, hoping they would steer your uncle's path. When he came to me for my blessing once he stole the throne, I told him it was he who set The Shadow in motion, for he would never receive my blessing. You, little flame, are of kind heart. You have the same hope and intentions as your parents, but you were not made for battle. I sent him to you so you could be free to care for your people. Free to help them. Allow The Shadow to do what needs to be done. The Shadow will always find you in your time of need."

She gently placed a kiss on my forehead, and bright light filled the room. I shut my eyes tight to shield myself from it. When the light dimmed, I opened my eyes and saw Rae smiling at me.

"Welcome back, my queen," she said with a bow.

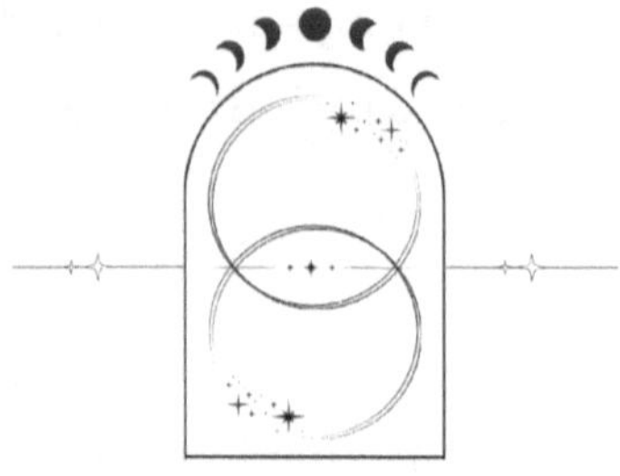

Fifteen

Lady Rae and I returned to the suite. As soon as we opened the door, Jax ran to me and wrapped me tight in his arms. Stella was sitting on the couch with a nervous expression, and as Rae went to her side, Stella stood. The two of them whispered to each other.

"I was so worried they were taking you from me," he said softly with concerned, stormy gray eyes before gently placing a kiss on my head.

"No one will ever take me from you, or you from me," I whispered back. I then told him of all that had happened in my time while I was gone. Jax stared down at me in shock as the story unfolded.

"My Queen," Lady Stella said with a bow. "Please allow me to guide you to the next part of your journey."

Jax finally released me, and we turned toward the Ladies of the Flame

"Please rise," I said, and she did. It felt so odd making such commands. I was Queen, but it still felt awkward. "I need to go to the palace. I cannot ask you to leave The Glade and travel all that way."

"The door downstairs leads to tunnels that will take you to the castle," Rae responded. "Stella will take you to them once you are ready."

"I didn't know there were tunnels," I said, confused.

"It was how your father and mother traveled back and forth to see each other during their courtship. It was originally placed as an emergency route, and is a well-kept secret," Rae said.

"Kept even from King Joffrey," Stella added. "We know that it will take you to the castle, but we are not exactly sure where. We believe there are several exits."

"Give us another day to prepare," Jax inserted himself. "I need to teach our fire queen how to blend into the shadows."

"If the queen agrees." Rae's gaze shot to me, and I gave her a nod of approval. "So it shall be. We will be here tomorrow at first light." The two Ladies exited the suite and shut the door behind them.

"We have lots of things to go over, especially if we are going to make it out alive," Jax said, turning to me.

"Killing a king is no joke. I have also never done a job with someone tagging along who I had to babysit."

"You do not need to babysit me!" I crossed my arms as I looked up at him and furrowed my brow.

His eyes darkened. "Yes, I do. I cannot allow any harm to come of you. You are my number one priority. Besides, are you going to be able to defend yourself if you're attacked?"

"I can defend myself!"

In an instant, Jax grabbed both of my wrists with one hand and slammed me into the wall with his blade to my throat. "You're dead if this happens to you in the castle."

"That wasn't fair! I was not expecting that." I squirmed in his grip, trying to get away.

"That's the point, *my queen*. You need to be ready for anything." He held me tighter and put his face an inch from mine. The air electrified around us. "If you want to get free, fight for it."

"Jax! Let go. I don't want to hurt you."

"Hurt me, princess. I dare you," he teased.

Heat flared in my body, and I focused my royal flames on him. His hands caught fire, but he didn't react. I sent more fire, but still, he acted as if nothing had happened.

"Is that all the fire queen has?" The smirk on his face grew. "What a shame. I expected more."

I forced all of my magic out of me and set all of him ablaze. He released me and stepped back with a confused expression, but he didn't react to the heat. I quickly extinguished the flames and noticed the ground was charred where he stood. He leaned down and dragged his finger against the black floor, inspecting it closely.

"Interesting..." he whispered. "I thought it had no heat, but it seems it did, and I am not affected by your flames."

"You felt nothing?" I asked, kneeling to meet his gaze.

"Nothing at all. What an interesting discovery." Jax raised his gaze to me. "Let's work on your stealth skills."

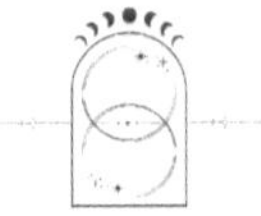

The next morning came too fast. Jax and I had stayed up halfway through the night, preparing for what was to come. When my head finally hit the pillow, I tossed and turned. My mind raced with every possible outcome, and I feared we were headed to our deaths.

Rolling onto my side, I faced Jax, who had not yet awoken. He looked so peaceful, and I found myself wondering what he was dreaming about. How could he sleep with what loomed on the horizon? I snuggled into him and inhaled his smokey, citrus scent. He wrapped his arms around me and ran his fingers through my hair.

"Good morning," he said with a yawn.

"Good morning. Lady Stella should be here any minute."

"Well then, we have another minute to do this." He gently lifted my chin and planted a kiss on my lips.

Just as we parted, there was a knock on the door. With a chuckle, Jax got out of bed, threw on his pants, and left the room. I got up to get ready for the day. After a few moments, Jax returned to the bedroom.

"Stella will wait for us downstairs."

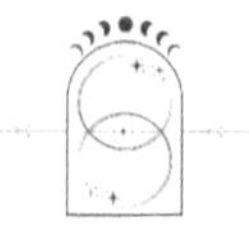

Luckily, my father had a stash of weapons for Jax to select from. Once we were geared up, the two of us met Stella in the foyer. She paced back and forth, and as soon as we came downstairs, she ran over to us.

"Good morning, my Queen." She smiled at me, then turned her attention to Jax. "Shadow," she said with a small nod of acknowledgment. "Please come this way."

She led us down the stairs and unlocked the door. Quickly, she ushered us inside and shut the door behind her. We were surrounded by total darkness. Jax took my hand and squeezed it as if he could sense my unease.

Lady Stella whispered something in the ancient fae language, and the torches lit up one by one, illuminating the long hallway before us.

"The flames will guide your way. No matter what, trust their guidance. For one wrong turn could mean your death," she said in a hushed tone as she paled.

"Our death?" Jax asked.

She nodded. "This tunnel was used for emergencies. Unwanted visitors would end up getting lost and disposed of. Please stay safe. Reclaim your throne. Save us. I beg of you."

"I promise. His reign ends here. I will restore Irolyth to the great land it once was."

Lady Stella did not say another word. She gave a quick nod, opened the door, and exited it. After it shut, the hall echoed with a locking sound, leaving Jax and I alone to finish our journey.

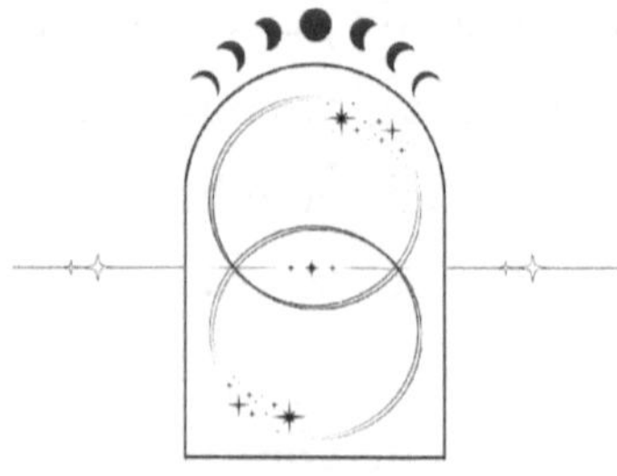

Sixteen

We had been walking for what seemed like hours down the cement hallways. The only guide is the iron torch-es hanging on the wall. The more we traveled, the farther apart they became. When we approached an intersection, each way had one torch. They remained unlit until we were upon them, and only one would light. When we made the turn, it would extinguish. A heavy must filled the air. The sounds of scratching, screams, and footsteps could be heard every so often, making me jump. Jax never faltered and kept his hand wrapped around mine. Fear tore through my body as a roar echoed off the walls, and I froze in place. There was no way I could do this. I can't face my uncle. I can't save Irolyth. Jax turned to me and gave me a reassuring kiss. "You're okay. Remember what Lady Stella said, just follow the flames."

I looked up at him and felt tears well in my eyes. Anxiety rattled my bones. It was all becoming too real. "Jax," I whimpered. "I don't think I can do this. I can't be queen. I can't kill my uncle. I can't find my way out of the darkness!"

He brushed away my tears with his thumb as determination filled his eyes. "You will be a wonderful queen. The Mother gave you her blessing for a reason. You will not kill that son of a bitch. I will. I will make him pay for everything he has put you through. We will get out of the darkness together." His voice rose as he spoke. "We will do this together." Then he spoke to me in a soft, calming voice. "The Fire Queen and her Shadow."

"You promise?"

He nodded. "I promise. With every fiber of my soul. We will make it out. I will kill him. You will be queen."

I wrapped him in a tight hug, and he returned the gesture. We stood there for a long moment, embracing one another. My breathing steadied, and the tears stopped flowing. The air in the tunnels changed, and a cold wind hit my back. Another loud roar filled my ears, and the ground shook. Jax's body tensed for a moment before he pulled away from me. He grabbed my wrist and pulled me into a sprint.

"Run! Don't look behind you!" He commanded.

I couldn't help but look and saw a large beast chasing after us. The bipedal monster was quickly closing the gap, but all I could focus on was the foam pouring out of its mouth and coating its long fangs. Jax yanked on my arm.

"Piper! I told you not to look!"

I turned my head back, facing forward once again, and pushed my short legs to run as fast as they could. The sound of our footsteps was swallowed by the beast's roars. Torches continued to light as we made our way through the halls. After what seemed like an eternity, the hallway suddenly split into two paths, but neither torch lit. Jax and I froze, gasping for air, and turned toward the beast barreling toward us.

"Well, Fire Queen, time to put that name to the test," Jax said as he readied his blade.

Heat filled my body as I focused on calling my magic. My eyes locked onto the beast's golden eyes with slitted pupils. I raised my hand, and fire formed in my palm. I hurled my flame at the monster, hit it in the shoulder, and caused it to stagger back.

The space darkened, and I noticed Jax was gone. When he reappeared, he was on the monster's back, plunging his dagger into its eye. It screamed and shook, raising its arm and trying to swipe its long claws over its shoulder. Jax vanished before contact could be made, leaving his dagger stuck in the monster's eye.

The beast ripped out the dagger and threw it toward me. I ducked and heard it clatter on the ground behind me. I barely had time to stand before the beast had closed the distance between us and backhanded me with its massive paw, sending me flying into the wall. I let out a scream on impact, felt as if my bones cracked, and then used what little strength I had left to cast another fireball. It hit dead center in the monster's chest, causing its fur to set ablaze.

A blade pierced through its stomach, and the beast's mouth pooled with blood. The blade was pulled out of the beast, and the monster fell to the ground, revealing Jax with a sword in hand. The fire roared and engulfed the beast entirely. After a moment, it was nothing but ash.

Jax dropped the weapon and rushed to me, fell to his knees, and cradled my face in his hands. Worry filled those stormy eyes. " Are you alright?" Panic rose in his voice.

"I... I am alright," I groaned. My body ached from being thrown into the wall, but it was nothing that wouldn't heal quickly.

A flash of bright light filled my vision. One of the directions in the forked hall had lit up, illuminating a dark wooden door up ahead. The gold Rossi family crest glittered in the firelight.

I was home.

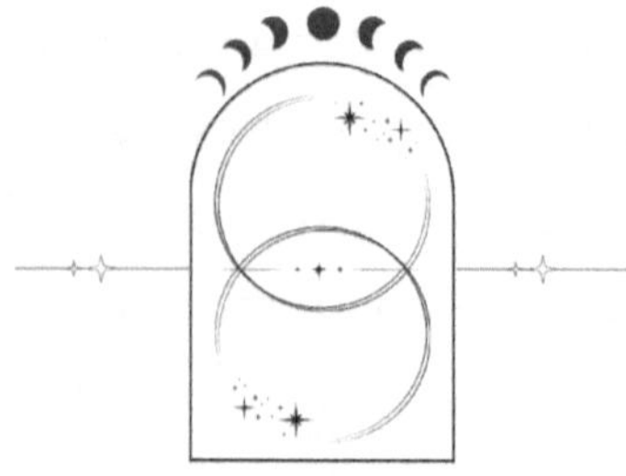

Seventeen

Before we opened the door, I threw on my glamour. Jax opened the door, and on the other side was a small, dust-filled square room with an iron ladder leading to a hatch on the ceiling. Jax put his finger to his lips, then went ahead of me. Unsheathing his blade, he put the steel between his teeth. After testing the stability of the ladder, he slowly climbed the rungs and cautiously lifted the hatch. He silently motioned for me to wait here. Then he vanished into the shadows, and the hatch shut.

Silence hung in the air and uneasiness settled in my core. Left to my own devices, my thoughts raced. I wondered where we were. If we were in the castle, where? What was beyond this room? What was Jax facing alone?

My stomach turned as I thought of what lay ahead. I thought of what The Mother had told me. I would not be a queen of violence. The Shadow would be my sword. Something in me cracked when I thought of forcing Jax to do terrible things on my behalf.

Was it forcing if he was already doing those things long before our paths crossed?

The hatch swung open, causing me to nearly jump out of my skin. Jax poked his head through the space. "Come on up. The coast is clear."

Once I was through the hatch, I knew exactly where we were. Dust gathered on the shelves of the pantry of our townhome in the city of Mayrin. I was surprised, as I thought the tunnels were to take us to the castle. My family and I would spend a week here every year in the winter for the Festival of Fire; a celebration held on the Winter Solstice.

In the center of the city, we would light a large fire to banish away the long nights and the cold weather. Once the fire was lit, the celebration would last for three days. There were so many street vendors, artists, and performances. It had been one of my favorite festivals.

"Do you know where we are?" Jax asked softly.

I gave him a nod. "This was our home in the city." The row of townhomes was against the wall that surrounded the palace grounds, and only nobility lived there.

"I searched the entire place. It's empty."

The two of us exited the pantry and entered the kitchen. I squinted from the bright sun shining through the dusty windows. When he said empty. He wasn't wrong. All furniture and decor had been removed from the entire house. A surreal feeling took over me. How could a place once filled with so much life be so dead?

"Are you ready to go into the city? Do you think you could get us into the castle from here?" Jax asked.

I turned my head to him and looked at him nervously. "I'm not sure. Maybe we should check the castle wall and see if there are any spots we can get through."

He stood there for a moment with a look of contemplation. "I think we need to see what type of guard presence is throughout the city first. We need to see exactly what's causing the people to run to The Glade. Once we know how many guards are around, we can plan our next move."

I nodded. The Mother knew exactly what she was doing when she put the two of us together. I needed someone who understood strategy. I needed someone to guide me through these hard times. I needed Jax.

We both agreed venturing out after sundown would be the best time to explore the city and begin our plan. There would be fewer people in the streets, and hopefully darkness would hide us. Until then, we would rest. We went back into the pantry and down the hatch to the empty room. The more hidden we were, the better.

The two of us sat on the ground with our backs against the wall. Jax wrapped his arm around me and pulled me close. I rested my head against his shoulder, and within the comfort of his arms, I fell asleep.

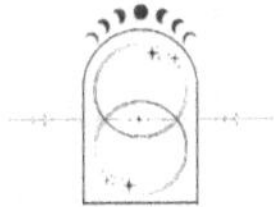

Loud voices jolted me awake, and I noticed Jax wasn't with me anymore. Climbing the ladder, I entered the pantry. The door that led to the kitchen was open. The space was filled with bright orange light. It must be sunset.

Voices chanted something I couldn't make out. Walking into the kitchen, I noticed Jax crouching by one of the windows. His eyes went wide when he saw me.

"Get down!" He commanded in a hushed tone.

I did, and he motioned for me to come over to him. Crawling across the kitchen floor, I joined him under the window.

"What's going on?" I asked.

"War." The coldness of his voice sent a shiver down my spine.

A loud boom filled my ears and rattled the house. The voices started chanting louder, and I was finally able to decipher what they were saying.

"Join the flame or be swallowed by it."

My heart sank as I peeked through the window. It was not the orange glow of sunset that had filled the room. Flames had engulfed large sections of the city. The streets were filled with guards. Some rushed toward the fires, others guided citizens into carriages.

"Don't even think about it," Jax snarled.

"What if those are our way into the castle?" I asked, pointing to the carriages.

"And what if they are to be set ablaze?"

"Fire can't hurt the Fire Queen and her Shadow," I responded with a grin as I jumped up. Before Jax could say anything, I glamoured myself into appearing as a guardswoman. In a flash, I was outside and in the center of the chaos. Jax rushed out of the house behind me.

A rough man's male voice grated in my ears. "Oi! Grab that man! He knows the rules. Anyone out past curfew is to be sent to the dungeons!"

"Yes, sir!" I grabbed Jax and guided him to the carriages.

"This is the stupidest thing you've ever done," he whispered so softly only I could hear.

A tall female guard approached us as we neared the carriages. "Throw him into this one. You will be the lucky one to drive it in. The previous driver got stabbed by one of the prisoners." She pointed over to a carriage. A man in the guard uniform laid on the ground in a pool of his own blood. "It's full once you add that one. You are good to go." She took a step closer. "What a shame too, because this one is interesting looking. Hopefully, the king won't send him immediately to his death."

With her final word, I pushed Jax toward the carriage. Rage boiled inside me. It took everything I had not to set all of the guards aflame and liberate the city, but I needed to stick to the plan. Another guard unlocked and opened the door. Once I forced Jax inside, the guard slammed the door shut and locked it. I walked to the front of the carriage, sat in the coach box, and drove it toward the castle, following the other carriages.

Panic welled in my mind as we passed through the gates. I tried to focus on the two black horses leading the carriage to calm my nerves.

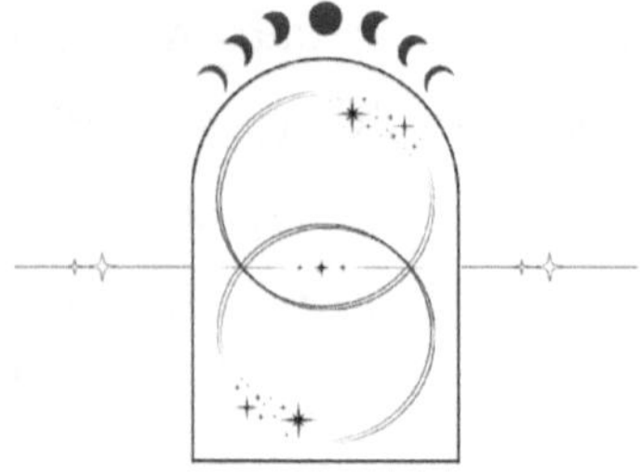

Eighteen

As soon as I stopped the horses next to the dungeon entrance, several guards rushed to the carriage. Prisoners were ushered out of the back of the carriage and led through a door leading to the dungeons. One of the guards pointed me in the direction of where to park the carriage and yelled for me to go down into the dungeons once I was done.

Doing as I was told, I parked the carriage and then made my way down to the dungeon. I was shocked no one had asked questions about a guard they had never seen before. My mind raced with all the things I had just seen. Anger continued to build in me. How could Joffrey treat the kingdom this way? How could he set the city ablaze and take his people prisoner?

Frigid air surrounded me as I descended the stairs and entered the dungeon. Both sides of the hall were cells filled with men, women, and children. My heart broke as I stared at their shivering bodies. Many had their ribs visible through their skin. I avoided their gazes. It took everything I had not to allow the tears to fall. I needed to find Jax and get us into the main section of the castle.

"You!" A deep voice shouted. I looked up and saw a large man in a captain's uniform. "Come with me."

A chill ran down my spine as he commanded me. I gave him a nod and said, "Yes, sir," trying to hide the shaking in my voice.

He guided me into a side room where a man sat tied to a chair with a burlap bag over his head. The captain walked over and ripped off the bag, revealing the man's bruised and bloody face. He looked defeated, and there was no light in his eyes. "This man was said to have been seen with a red-haired woman. He is refusing to give us any information." The captain grabbed the prisoner by the hair and yanked his head back. "My hope is that he will tell us something today."

"I told you, there was no red-haired woman!" The prisoner spat.

"You lie!" the captain spat back and punched the captive in the jaw.

My heart pounded in my chest as I watched the captain assault the man. He did not deserve this. All for being thought to be seen with me. After three years, Joffrey still sought me and punished anyone even rumored to have been seen with me. Fury burned in my heart until it morphed into hot determination. I was the key to ending all this pain.

Just as the captain's fist almost met with the man's face again, I yelled, "Stop!"

The captain quickly turned to me with anger in his eyes. "Did you just give me an order?"

"Yes, I did," I snarled. "As your queen, I command you to stop. I command all of you to stop!" My voice raised with every word. It was now or never. I needed to end this. Jax would find me later. The Shadow always followed the flame.

"Oh, you think just because the king brought you to his bed that means something? News flash, sweetheart, he brings all women who work in the castle to his bed." The captain walked toward me, and I held his rage-filled gaze.

"My name is Piper Camilla Rossi, the rightful Queen of Irolyth." I dropped my glamour, and a fireball formed in my hand. "Take me to my uncle."

His eyes widened, but his look of shock quickly turned to one of hatred. "You made a grave mistake, *princess*. You really think you're coming out of this alive?" The captain snarled at me.

"I know I will," I said with all the confidence I had left. "The Mother gave me her blessing. I will not disappoint her."

He laughed. "Turn around. There are four guards blocking your path. Do you really think you can take all five of us?"

"How about we even the score?" A familiar voice filled my ears as Jax stepped out of the shadows and ran a blade across the captain's throat. My Shadow raised his gaze to look beyond me. "Are you ready to meet the same end as your captain?"

The guards gathered at the door looked on in horror. Without hesitating, I quickly threw fire at their feet, causing them to shout in panic and disperse. I did not want to kill anyone who did not deserve it. For all I knew, they were forced to follow their king's orders under penalty of death. Learning who was truly on Joffrey's side would need to come after I reclaimed my throne.

"Come on. We have to run!" I said to Jax before rushing out of the room. The two of us raced through the halls. Finally, we neared the door leading into the main section of the castle. A large man blocked our path with a great axe in hand. Before I could even stop to face him, two daggers flew past me and hit him in his eyes. The man screamed and staggered, falling to the ground.

We ran past his prone body, up the steps, and entered the main castle. It was cold and dark. Not a single sconce on the wall was lit. Jax slammed the door shut and slid a piece of furniture in front of it so no one could follow us through.

"You stupid girl," he growled at me. "Do you have any idea how reckless all of that was? What if I hadn't been there?" He caged me against the wall. My back pressed into the cold stone.

"I knew you would be." I stood my ground.

"How? How could you have known?" He leaned in close.

"Because where there is the flame..."

Before I could finish the sentence, he continued, "there is the shadow. When I was underwater, that phrase was repeated over and over. And when I was taken into the dungeons, I knew exactly what room to wait for you in."

A smile crossed my face. "You will always find me when I need you."

"Because you are mine. Mine to protect. Mine to cherish. Mine to serve. I don't know why The Mother connected us, but I am so glad she did." He closed the gap between us and quickly kissed my lips. "But don't you ever do anything that stupid ever again."

"I cannot promise you that," I giggled.

A low orange glow filled the space, followed by a high-pitched scream. "Princess Piper?"

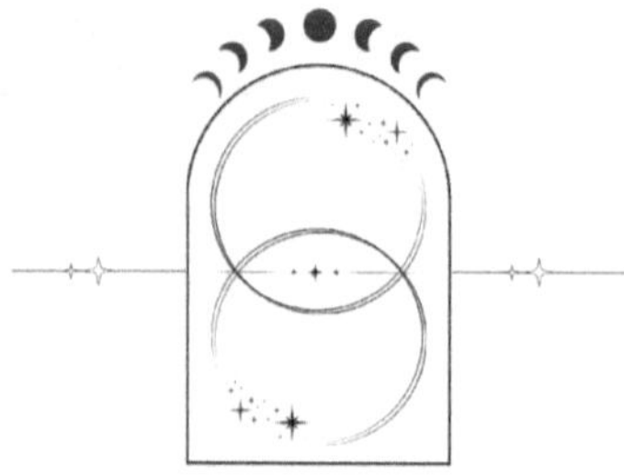

Nineteen

My head snapped in the direction of the sound as the woman dropped her torch onto the stone floor. My jaw dropped when I saw the sister of my lady's maid. Shock rattled through me. She looked so different than she did three years ago. Once plump and tan, she was now thin and sallow. The darkness under her eyes broke my heart. Her dress had tears along the hem.

"Mabel, is that really you?" My voice cracked as I spoke.

She ran to me and wrapped me in a hug. "Oh, thank The Mother. I thought you were dead."

I held her tight. "I am alive. I am well. I am here to save us all." Tears I could no longer hold back fell from my eyes.

"Who is this?" Jax questioned in a cold tone.

Mabel released me and gave Jax an up-and-down look. "A human? You brought a human here?"

"He's no human. He is The Shadow."

Mabel staggered back with a gasp and pulled me to her. "Mother, save us."

"The Mother sent him to me. Everything we learned about The Shadow was wrong," I said, hugging her back. "The only flame he is extinguishing is Joffrey's. Jax is my sword and shield. I would not be here without him." I pulled from her embrace and turned toward Jax. "Jax, this is Mabel. She was the sister to my lady's maid, Ingrid." Turning back to Mabel, I asked her, "Is Ingrid still here? I can't wait to see her!"

Mabel hung her head. "She was hung a week after you vanished. The king was convinced she knew your whereabouts."

My eyes went wide, and my body shuddered. "No," I rasped. "No!"

"Unfortunately so, my Lady. Come, let's get you out of these halls before someone else sees you."

Mabel guided us down the hallways and some stairs into the servant's quarters. Once a clean area hosting many private rooms, the space was now filled with dust, and the walls had been knocked down to create one large room. Dirty and ruined bedrolls filled the floor. As I stood there, taking in the depressing sight,

Mabel told me Joffrey treated the people who worked in his castle like animals. Most of the workers were out doing their chores, as they were now done mostly at night to avoid the king. Only a few older ones remained in the quarters, curled up in their bedrolls. All of them had a horrid cough. Mabel informed us of how a deadly illness had quickly spread. Anyone who caught it was lucky to survive, as the servants were receiving no medical treatment. In the back of the room, there was a small hole in the wall. She ushered us in, ducking our heads to avoid the top of the opening, and we now stood in one of the secret passageways that were throughout the castle.

"When King Joffrey ordered the tearing down of the individual rooms, they made this hole in the wall. They did not care enough to fix it, nor did they think to check it." Mabel said with a smile.

"I am so sorry this has happened to you all. You know my father would have never stood for how you are being treated." I gave her another hug.

"Oh, my sweet princess, I know. I was always grateful for how your parents treated us all as equals, no matter our position. And I know once you are on the throne, you will restore our dignity. Now please, go. Down this way." She pointed to the left. "This will lead you to his throne room. Around this time, he sits there and has the servants worship him." A disgusted look took over her face. "Kill him and save us all."

She squeezed me tight before releasing me. We said our goodbyes, and she exited through the hole in the wall. I turned back to Jax with a fire in my eyes.

I would save them.

I would restore peace to Irolyth.

I would be the Queen they deserved.

"Are you ready?" Jax asked, with a look of determination on his face.

"Born ready." I gave him a quick nod.

The two of us quickly traveled down the dark pathway. I had summoned a fireball to light our way. After what seemed like an eternity, we came to a dead end. It would be an impasse for anyone who did not understand how the secret tunnels worked. Ingrid and I used to play hide and seek throughout them my entire childhood. I walked over to the wall and pressed on the center stone. The wall popped outward and slid open to reveal the back of the throne.

Where once sat two thrones, now there was only one. The memory of my mother just tossed. Joffrey thought of us as disposable to his plans.

Today would be the last time he would tarnish my family's name.

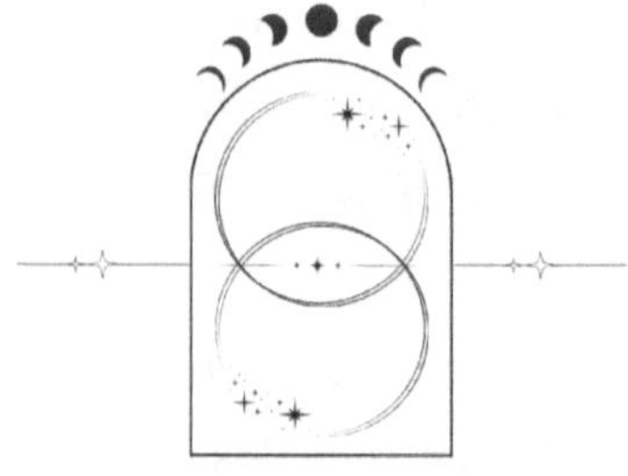

Twenty

"Hello, uncle. Remember me?" I snarled.

Joffrey jumped up from the throne and spun toward us. His eyes went wide, and his face paled. The servant woman who had been kneeling before him rushed out of the room, leaving the three of us alone.

I stepped out of the secret pathway with Jax behind me. Joffrey's eyes met mine, and we stared at each other in silence. He was nearly skin and bones, and his skin had grown so pale. His once long, red hair and beard were now white as snow, but his emerald eyes were still as piercing as I remembered them to be. I wondered how someone could deteriorate so vastly in only three years.

"I know it must hurt seeing the face of your 'favorite niece' after all this time." Anger burned through me as all the lies he told me ran through my mind. How he loved me. How he loved my brother. How he loved my parents. How everything he did was to serve the crown and the people of Irolyth.

His face soured. "Piper, after all this time. After all the searching I have done, what a surprise to have you come to me." Venom dripped off his words.

"I have come to reclaim my throne. You have brought Irolyth to ruin, and I intend to restore it to its former glory."

Jax placed his hand on my shoulder. A silent reminder he was here to support me. Behind me, every step of the way as my Shadow.

"No." He clicked his tongue. "You have come to die, and when you do, The Mother will finally bless me with the royal flames. I will burn Irolyth to the ground, and a new Irolyth will rise from the ashes."

"The Mother will never give you her blessing. Irolyth was thriving before you framed my father and had him hung!"

"Irolyth was weak! Klaus and I had a vision for Irolyth! It all went out the window when he met your mother and allowed her to make him weak. He was too worried about harmony that he didn't see the signs of contempt brewing. He didn't see the nobles were unsettled by the policies he set in place. He didn't see I was his enemy."

"Don't you dare speak ill of my father. The only mistake he ever made was sparing you when he won the crown. Do you want to know what I see? I see you are a monster. That you destroyed our once beautiful land and people. I see how you are weak and your reign is over. I see it all. What I have planned for you isn't punishment enough. You deserve to suffer the way the people of Irolyth have suffered."

Joffrey laughed. "It seems your friend has abandoned you. The man just vanished into..." he trailed off, and fear and realization grew in his eyes. "No. It can't be."

I smirked. "Vanished into *what*, dear uncle?" I asked in an innocent tone.

Joffrey spun on his heels and ran. I waved my hand in the air and brought up a wall of fire in front of him, forcing him to stagger and fall onto his bottom.

"What happened to you?" I asked. "When I last saw you, you were strong. But now you are nothing more than a frail old man. I almost feel bad I am about to destroy someone so pathetic. Allowing you to meet your end is a mercy. A mercy you don't deserve."

Joffrey quickly stood and faced me. "You! *You* are what happened to me. All because I didn't kill you. I made a pact with a demon. I promised him the royal family's souls in exchange for the royal flames and power. It was he who set the sanctuary aflame three years ago that set everything in motion. Since my bargain was incomplete, he slowly took my soul from me. You ruined everything!" He lunged at me, but before he could take a second step Jax reappeared in front of him.

Joffrey pulled a dagger from his waistband and stabbed at Jax. In one quick movement, Jax grabbed my uncle's wrist and twisted it. Joffrey let out a cry and the dagger fell to the floor. Jax kicked it away and vanished once again into the shadows.

"No." I shook my head, and Jax reappeared by my side. "You did. You ruined everything, including yourself," I said in a soft tone.

A fireball formed in my hand, and I hurled it toward Joffrey. He screamed and wailed as he burned and withered to ash. By betraying our family, he refused to join the flame, and in the end, was consumed by it.

Tears fell down my face. After all this time, it was finally over.

Jax pulled me into his chest, and I fell against him, sobbing. He held me tight and smoothed the back of my hair and kissed the top of my head. "It's over. It's over. You are safe. You freed Irolyth."

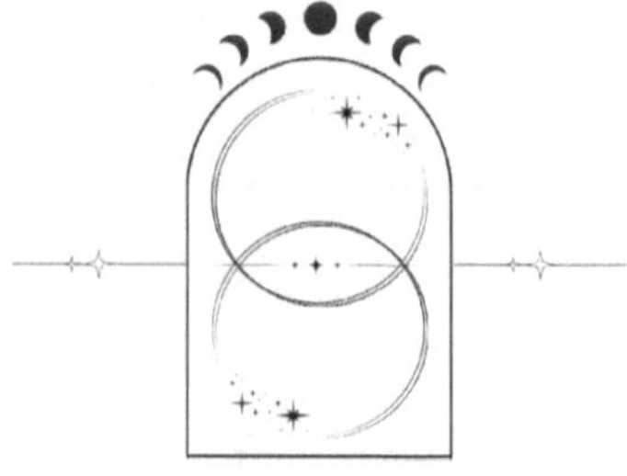

Twenty-One

Three months later, I had successfully rebuilt the capital city of Mayrin. All the refugees from The Glade had moved back, and things were finally beginning to feel normal. Jax removed any guards who had the same ideals and values as my uncle. The castle workers were given time off to rest so I could have the quarters renovated to what they once were. I also made sure that any who had fallen ill received proper treatment.

I sat in my bed and stared out the window, watching the sunrise. Never did I think I would be back in my old room. It seemed as if I had lived so many lives between that fateful day three years ago to now. Jax was staying in my brother's room. The two of us spent most of our free time together, but since becoming queen, there was little free time to be had.

Jax had left on business three days ago. He and I had an agreement I would not ask him what kind of business he had. As my Shadow, I expected him to do some unsavory things on my behalf for the best of the kingdom. He promised me after taking out my uncle, I would never have to do anything like that ever again.

He also promised he would be back before tonight, and I hoped that to be true.

A small knock sounded on my door. "My queen, it's me. May I come in?" Mabel asked.

"Come in."

"Happy coronation day!" She said as she brought in a tray full of food. She sat it down on the bedside table, and I took note of the coffee and apple pastries. Taking a deep breath, I inhaled the aromas. Mabel sat on the edge of my bed. "Are you excited?"

"I have been queen for three months. I'm not sure a party is necessary or appropriate now."

"It most certainly is! If anyone deserves a party, it is you. The people of Irolyth also need some joy after what we have endured." She jumped up from the bed and set the table next to the window. "Now, make sure you eat up. You won't be able to eat again until the feast tonight. I made sure to grab all your favorites: apple pastries, bacon, poached eggs, grapes, and peaches!"

"Thank you, Mabel." I offered her a smile as I got out of bed and sat at the table. "Has Jax returned?"

"Not yet. I am sure he will be back before the party!"

I let out a sigh and took a sip of the coffee. "Run through the agenda for today," I said.

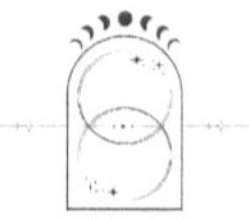

I knelt before the throne. The room looked vastly different than it had when I battled Joffrey. He had kept the room so bare. Now, there are floral arrangements, statues, and paintings. Lady Rae stood in front of me, holding a golden crown with rubies on the tips in her hand. My head was bowed as she spoke in the ancient language. A language that, for the past three months, I had been struggling to learn. Typically, only the line of succession was taught the language. Since I was never meant to be queen, I was not offered those lessons.

"Queen Piper Camilla Rossi," she said in the common tongue. "Blessed by The Mother, and savior of Irolyth. I bestow upon you the crown." She placed the crown on my head. "Long live the Queen."

"Long live the Queen!" The crowd erupted behind me.

I slowly stood and turned to them with a wide smile. "Thank you. I will spend my entire life continuing to prove I am worthy of this land, its people, and its throne. Let the festivities begin!"

On my final word, music filled the hall, and everyone began dancing. I looked around the room, trying to find Jax. Trying not to show my disappointment, I stepped down from the dais and made my way over to the table lined with drinks and food.

Before I made it to the table, a dark voice purred in my ear. "My queen, you look stunning in that dress." Jax stood in a black suit with golden trim. His tie was the same shade of red as my dress.

"I was beginning to worry you weren't going to make it!"

"I wouldn't miss this for the world. Come, I have a surprise for you." He took me by the hand and guided me through the crowd. We exited the throne room and entered the courtyard. In the center was a gazebo with two people standing in the center.

My jaw dropped as I recognized them. I lifted my dress and sprinted toward my friends, who met me halfway. The three of us entered a huge embrace.

Steph laughed. "Being queen looks good on you."

"I can't believe you never told me you are fae!" Steve added.

"I missed you guys so much. You have no idea." I turned back to Jax and smiled. "Thank you."

"Did you think I would let you experience your big day without your best friends?"

The three of us caught up on everything that had happened over the last three months. Stephanie had sold The White Rabbit to Steve. I had inspired her to return to her roots as well. She had heard of a sorceress who lived in the northern island, Varia, that may be related to her and she planned to find her.

Once we were caught up, I took Jax by his hand. He gave it a gentle squeeze and a cocky grin grew on his face.

"Would you give me the honor of dancing with me?" He asked.

I got up on my tippy toes and gave him a soft kiss. "I thought you would never ask."

The four of us walked back inside, and we joined in the celebration.

The celebration of Irolyth.

The celebration of life.

The celebration of The Fire Queen and her Shadow.

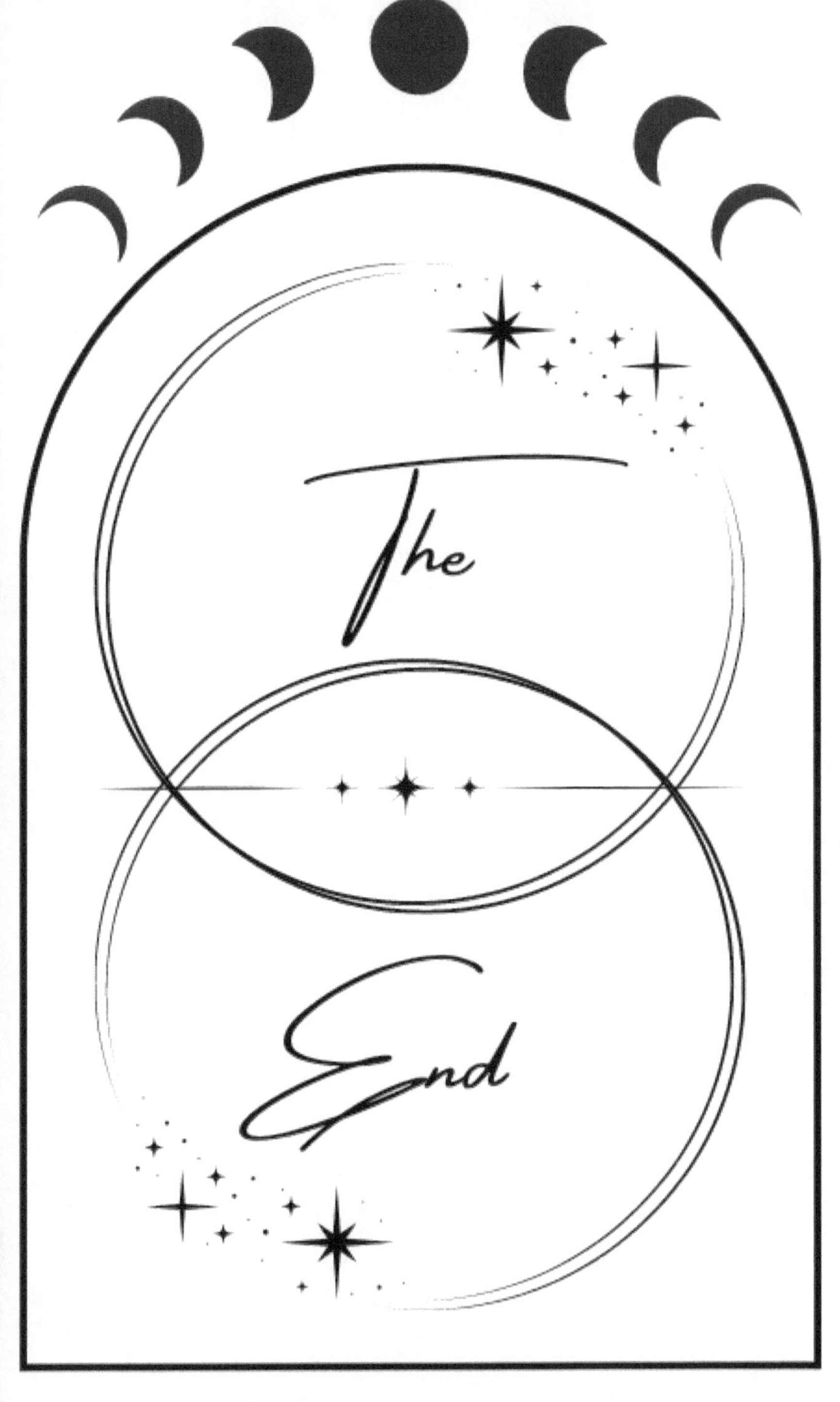
The
End

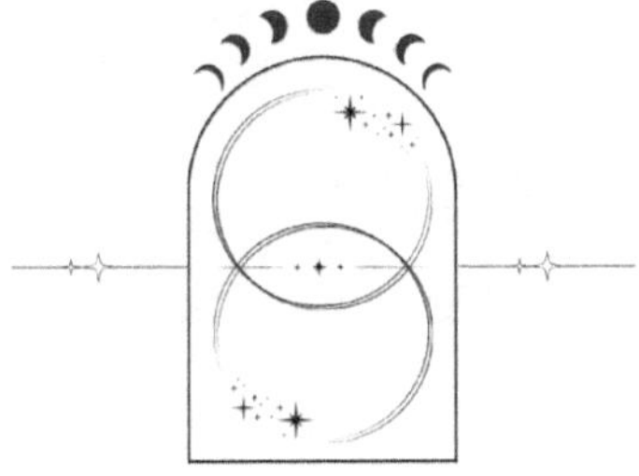

Also by Willow Asteria

The Blood Singer Trilogy
https://amzn.to/3KO4erc

The Realms of Elswyth
https://amzn.to/3xsvM2r

Learn More Here!